THE
HELIUM
MURDER

THE
HELIUM
MURDER

•

Camille Minichino

AVALON BOOKS
THOMAS BOUREGY AND COMPANY, INC.
401 LAFAYETTE STREET
NEW YORK, NEW YORK 10003

© Copyright 1998 by Camille Minichino
Library of Congress Catalog Card Number 98-96072
ISBN 0-8034-9298-7

THIRD PRINTING

PRINTED IN THE UNITED STATES OF AMERICA
ON ACID-FREE PAPER
BY HADDON CRAFTSMEN, BLOOMSBURG, PENNSYLVANIA

To my husband and greatest supporter, Richard Rufer, and my cousins Gloria, Jean, and Yolanda

Acknowledgments

My thanks to the many relatives and friends who have helped me with this manuscript, especially Robert Durkin, Ellen Patey, Sue Stephenson, and Penny Warner. I'm very grateful also for the wonderful support from Marcia Markland and the staff at Avalon Books.

Prologue

Congresswoman Margaret Hurley has a lot on her mind as she drives her rented Honda through icy streets toward the Whitestone home in Revere, Massachusetts. Among more serious matters, like how to survive the holidays with her impossible brother, and a showdown with her ex-fiancé, she toys with the issue of more snowplows for this city where she grew up.

As she strains her long, thin neck for the best view through the streaky windshield and tightens her grip on the steering wheel, Margaret is also thinking of helium.

If she were in her own car, she thinks, a more substantial Lincoln Continental, she'd reach down and start the tape recorder. For now, she has to be content with mental lists.

Number one, talk to Frances Whitestone, her chief benefactor and mentor, about the helium reserves.

Number two, visit Vinnie Cavallo at the lab on Charger Street and check on the progress of his report. Unless Vinnie has a big surprise, she's determined to vote to sell the government's reserve: thirty-two billion cubic feet of helium now stockpiled in a gas field near Amarillo, Texas. Margaret smiles as she thinks of the dumb but irresistible jokes about how many party balloons does a country really need?

Number three, meet with Bill Carey, the CEO of CompTech, and set him straight on his dealings with the helium storage program managers. Margaret glances at her briefcase on the floor of the passenger seat, as if she can see through the leather to the contracts inside.

Numbers four and five are the personal matters— try to reason with her brother Buddy, maybe get him some help for his gambling addiction; and confront Patrick Gallagher, whose latest hobby seems to be calling and writing Margaret with reminders of their warlike relationship.

Margaret stops at a traffic light on Broadway, in front of Revere City Hall, grateful for a chance to relax her neck. In spite of her thick fleece-lined gloves, she manages a few finger exercises. She breathes deeply and catches a whiff of pine. The picture of a beautifully decorated Christmas tree comes to her mind before she realizes that the fragrance stems from the green cardboard air freshener hanging from the Honda's cigarette lighter.

Out of habit, Margaret checks her image in the rear-view mirror, knowing that she can count on Frances

Whitestone, still elegant at seventy-six years old, to comment on Margaret's out-of-control, frizzy red hair and the coffee stain on the front of her green loden jacket. But she realizes with relief that for a few days she doesn't have to struggle to look older than her thirty-four years, or bulkier than her one hundred and twenty pounds, to get the attention of her colleagues in the House of Representatives.

Margaret cracks her window open to hear the carolers on the corner. She smiles as she pulls away, imagining that the choir has materialized at the intersection of Broadway and Pleasant Street just for her, other drivers being too intelligent to be on the road under these conditions.

As she hits patches of ice along Broadway and skids around the corner onto Revere Street, she hears the jingle of the bells on the packages that fill two shopping bags in the backseat. With only two blocks to go, she feels a twinge of holiday spirit and swears she can smell pumpkin pie as she passes a bakery that's clearly sealed up for the night.

Just before eight o'clock, Margaret pulls up in front of the stately Whitestone home, a few blocks from St. Anthony's Church. She leans her forehead on the steering wheel and lets out a long sigh. The trip from Logan Airport has seemed longer than a Science and Technology Committee meeting.

Margaret is grateful for the strings of colored lights decorating almost every house on Oxford Park, the wide, oddly named, tree-lined street that Frances Whitestone lives on. She frowns as she notices that all the streetlights are out, and the tiny red and green holiday bulbs provide the only illumination. She grumbles about the city budget as she unfolds her tall frame from the small car and walks to the back with great care, her boots cracking ice under her feet, her neck freezing as her scarf flies loose of her collar. Her purse-sized flashlight creates an eerie oval patch in front of her, like a poor spotlight in a second-rate theater production.

Margaret pulls on the strap of her brown leather garment bag and has lifted it free of the trunk when she hears a thunderous noise. She turns to see blinding high beams of white light barrel down on her, then fade to black. Margaret clutches her luggage to her chest like a plate of armor. As her eyes recover, she tries to determine what kind of car or van has disturbed the peace of Oxford Park, as if that were her only problem as the vehicle heads straight for her.

By the time she understands what's happening, a ton of metal rams into her, slamming her into the trunk of the Honda, where she lands like a discarded laboratory specimen, her head pushed into the crack between the back of the car and the raised trunk, her legs hanging over the license plate at odd angles.

The vehicle screeches backwards, then roars away, leaving an ugly trail of exhaust and blood to pollute the falling snow. One final jingle from a tiny bell sounds from the backseat of the Honda as it recovers from its blow, settling again into stillness.

Chapter One

"It's a mystery," my best friend Rose said to me. "A grown woman. How can you not like shopping? Especially Christmas shopping?"

She stamped her tiny foot on the ground—to get rid of the snow, I hoped, and not to make a statement about my reluctance to go into one more store full of cartoon Santas and special deals on mitten-and-scarf sets. "It's a wonder we've stayed friends for fifty years."

"I think it's only forty-six years," I said, "and maybe we wouldn't still be friends if I hadn't lived three thousand miles away for more than thirty of them."

"No, no, don't say that, Gloria," Rose said. "I'm so glad you're back." And we hugged right there on the street. Our shopping bags twisted around each other; my new leather gloves fell into a pool of cold, slushy, brown water in the gutter; and we laughed like a couple of junior-high schoolgirls cutting history class together. If passing shoppers noticed our two short, middle-aged frames embracing—mine wide and soft, Rose's small and wiry—no one said anything.

With soft snow falling all around us on the streets of downtown Boston and bells ringing on every corner, I had to admit that shopping for Christmas presents was more fun than, say, sweeping broken glass from a laboratory floor.

"I think it's all those years you spent in a physics lab," Rose said. "It's not like you could browse through catalogs for hydrogen or spend a day at a helium sale."

"Now there's where you're wrong," I said, jumping at the chance to talk science, and impressed that she knew the first two elements of the periodic table. By now we'd arrived at the doorway of Filene's, famous for its many basement levels, with dramatic markdowns on each one, and I realized that Rose had used her small technical vocabulary to distract me so she could drag me inside. Rose and I often engaged in this unspoken trade-off. If she'd let me have my science fix, I'd follow her into a dressing room where she tried on her size sevens, or maybe I'd listen to a bit of gossip about our hometown of Revere, Massachusetts, a few miles north of Boston.

"First," I said, forging ahead in spite of the distractions of what seemed like tons of merchandise, "I did often browse through catalogs to purchase hydrogen—that's how I bought the gas tubes for my spectrum studies. And second, helium actually is now for sale—by the federal government.''

I guessed that Rose probably hadn't followed the debates in Congress about whether the United States government should ''be in the helium business,'' as they put it. I'd listened to the sessions on C-Span and agreed with those who favored keeping the helium the government has been collecting since the Kennedy Administration. Like them, I was concerned that in a few years helium would be rare and we wouldn't have enough for important applications, like magnetic imaging in hospitals or state-of-the-art upgrades for future transportation systems.

''Tell me more,'' Rose said, fingering a dark green silk scarf. ''What do you think?'' she asked, holding the scarf up to her hair, still a deep brown with red highlights, thanks to modern technology. Although I had enormous faith in science and had all sorts of electronic gadgetry in my life, my short, mostly gray hair was proof that I didn't trust chemistry as much as I did physics.

''I think I will tell you more,'' I said, ''as long as we're in this nice, warm store. There's an important vote coming up on the federal helium reserves. And before you make a joke about high-pitched giggles, let me point out that helium plays an important role in many industries, including medicine.''

I hoped I sounded appropriately reproachful, but it was lost on Rose.

''Gloria, you're home after spending half a lifetime in California,'' she reminded me. ''It's going to be a white Christmas, chestnuts are roasting right here on the street carts, and you even have a boyfriend. Forget helium. By the way, what are you going to get Matt for Christmas?''

''I was thinking of a nice shirt and tie.''

I pictured Sergeant Matt Gennaro at his desk, flipping through homicide files in a new pale blue shirt and perhaps a rakish paisley tie. I saw myself admiring the outfit as we lunched together at Russo's, around the corner from the old red-brick building that houses the Revere Police Department where Matt has spent his whole career.

''I'm not surprised,'' Rose said with a groan. She gave me a look of hopelessness. ''You keep forgetting, you're not only his science consultant anymore. You're his girlfriend. That was at least one good thing that came of those two awful murders last fall.''

''It's not that we're engaged either, Rose,'' I said. ''We're just starting to become friends.''

Another sigh from Rose. ''Still, here's your first serious relationship since 1963 and you're thinking of work clothes? A shirt and tie is what you should buy Frank,'' she said, referring to her husband of three decades and my good friend for as many years.

Rose and Frank were also my landlords for the six months that I'd been back in town. They'd set me up in an apartment above their place of business, so for the moment, my address was the same as the one in their yellow-pages ad: Galigani's Mortuary on Tuttle Street.

The Galiganis also sold me last year's Cadillac from

their fleet—a side benefit that took some getting used to. For the first few weeks, I'd arrived early for every gathering and parked in dark corners to avoid being seen behind the wheel of a long, black luxury car.

"How about something personal?" Rose said, bringing me back to the task of shopping. "It's a perfect time to show Matt you think of him more as a friend than a boss."

At the word "friend," Rose lifted her penciled-in dark brown eyebrows and puckered her lips, a gesture I tried to ignore. She picked a piece of white lint from my new winter coat, as if that was all it would take for me to look as stunning as she always did.

"What if I have his initials embroidered on the pocket of the shirt?"

"I was thinking more along the lines of a slow-dancing tape in the pocket of a bathrobe," Rose said, sending us into a preteen laughfest again.

Just to humor her, I let Rose take me through the men's department, past the ties, to the more personal aisles. Before she said anything out loud, I shook my head wildly when she pointed to a headless plastic torso wearing orange-and-black-tiger-striped underwear. Rose knew it would take more than one visit for me to be as comfortable in the menswear section as I would be in a hardware store, so she didn't press me to buy anything. However, I could tell from the slight smile on her well-made-up face that she was devising a plan for a future trip. As for me, I made a mental note to visit Radio Shack on my own.

* * *

We headed for the Park Street subway station, walking past a long row of newspaper vending machines. Rose was five feet ahead of me before she noticed that I'd stopped in front of a *Boston Globe* display. I was staring wide-eyed at the headline: *Seventh District Rep Hit-and-Run Victim.*

Rose joined me at the blue metal case that stood in front of us like a truncated TV anchorman announcing the day's bad news. Since neither of us had change, we leaned our shopping bags against the rack, and read as much as we could see of the folded front page.

Congresswoman Margaret Hurley died late last night of injuries sustained after a vehicle ran her down in front of the old Whitestone home in Revere. Neither Mrs. Whitestone, longtime supporter of Hurley's career, nor Hurley's brother were available for comment. Police have no witnesses to what appears to be a random hit-and-run.

''Wow,'' Rose said. ''Whitestone lives in that beautiful white house on Oxford Park, the one that has green shutters with shamrock cutouts.''

''I know the one you mean,'' I said, still stooped over, ''only because it was the only non-Italian symbol in that neighborhood.''

''I remember when Margaret was elected to Congress, two years ago, largely due to the widow Whitestone, by the way, but we didn't know her very well. Did you?''

I straightened up with a jolt, when I finally remembered why her name was familiar.

''She's the helium vote,'' I said.

''She's the what?''

''She's on the House Science and Technology Committee. I wonder if her death had anything to do with the helium vote?''

''Oh-oh,'' Rose said. ''Here we go again.''

Chapter Two

Not that I didn't like my new career as science consultant to the Revere Police Department, but I needed a longer break after the last murder investigation I'd gotten involved in. That case was only two months earlier, and didn't end until I got my first taste of a bullet wound.

Back in my apartment after an afternoon of shopping with Rose, I rubbed my shoulder, not so much from residual pain as from the memory of wrestling with the murderer. Before I could get too upset, however, I realized that my boss and, as Rose would say, boyfriend, Sgt. Matt Gennaro, dealt with many more homicides than that. I was called in only if the murder involved science or scientists as suspects, like the case of the murdered hydrogen researchers I'd just helped with.

From the headlines, I had no reason to believe that

Hurley's death had anything to do with science, and I certainly didn't know her personally. So why was I giving this case a second thought? It was none of my business. It was a simple hit-and-run, I thought, as if random violence is any more simple to understand than premeditated murder.

This newest phase of my life had begun when I'd retired from my physics lab in California and returned to Revere, as abruptly as I'd left. It had been more than thirty years since my departure, right after my fiancé at that time, Al Gravese, died in a car crash. My plan, if I could call it that, was to see how it felt to be back in the city I was raised in.

I had some unanswered questions about Al's death, and any day now I was going to do something about the little notebook of his that I'd found in one of the cartons Rose and Frank had stored for me in their attic—now my attic, too.

My return to Revere also unleashed unresolved feelings centering around Josephine Lamerino, my mother and worst enemy in my formative years.

"You'll never amount to anything, Gloria," Josephine told me almost daily during the first twenty years of my life. *"You're fat and lazy."*

I'd expected her to stop taunting me when I did all my chores, or when I was valedictorian in high school, but she never did. Not even after she died, when I was in college—her voice never left my head. Josephine's early message to me was louder than that of my father, who whispered that he was proud of me; stronger than that of my professors as

I earned a Ph.D. in physics; more powerful than that of friends like Rose and Frank. It was my life's work to drown her out and build some measure of self-confidence.

My whistling kettle brought me back to the present. I settled in my favorite glide rocker with a mug of French-pressed coffee, which added as much rich aroma as good taste to my afternoon. I opened my copy of the *Boston Globe* and read the full article about Margaret Hurley. A sidebar about her career profiled Margaret as one of a new crop in the House of Representatives. At thirty-four years old, she was the elected spokesperson for the people of the Seventh Congressional District of Massachusetts, which included Revere.

I'd hoped for a reference to the helium vote, but the *Globe* reporter focused more on Hurley's personal life and overall professional accomplishments, noting that her minor in chemistry at Boston's Simmons College added value to her political science major, and got her a choice spot on the Science and Technology Committee. Hurley's only survivor was her brother, Brendan ''Buddy'' Hurley. No details of the accident, if that's what it was.

I wondered if Matt would see this death as science related and invite me to work on the case. I envisioned myself tutoring him on helium as I had on the hydrogen case. I thought I'd begin by emphasizing how difficult it is to capture helium in a useful form on earth, in spite of its abundance—hydrogen and helium together make up almost ninety-nine percent of the universe.

I mentally prepared a chart for Matt, showing him the uses of helium at various temperatures. I titled it, ''The Coldest Liquid in the Universe.''

The picture of us working together was very appealing. Matt was a widower, and eight months younger than me, as I'd found out during a spontaneous party for his fifty-fifth birthday in the fall. Was I actually looking for more police work? Or a way to spend more time with Matt? Neither motive was appealing to me, since I was still uncomfortable with this adventuresome life I seemed to have adopted recently.

I got busy at my computer, searching the Internet for information on who stood where in Congress on the helium vote. According to the sites I browsed, it seemed that Congress was leaning toward selling the reserves. I wondered how Hurley would have voted, resolving to check earlier newspapers for a clue as to which way she was leaning.

I'd just gotten a computer hit on a report submitted by a physicist, Vincent Cavallo, a consultant hired by the government to do an independent analysis of the program, when the phone rang.

''Hi, Glor. Any new murders lately?'' Elaine Cody, a technical editor at the lab I'd worked at for many years, was teasing me long distance, from her Berkeley, California, home.

Elaine and Rose had much in common, starting with

their wardrobes—designer suits and dresses, Italian leather handbags and pumps for work, and fancy sandals for evening. Even their sweat suits were plush and beautifully tailored. *No matter which coast I live on*, I thought, *my friends are thinner and classier than I am.*

Rose's husband Frank was also in that category, a natty dresser, staying fit and trim in spite of his healthy appetite for Italian food. So far, of all the people I was attracted to in one way or another, Matt Gennaro was the only one who looked like me—between two and three sizes overweight, with naturally graying hair and a closet full of dark clothes, designed to disappear into the wallpaper.

"I want to be like Marie Curie," I'd told Elaine once when she tried to persuade me to buy a frothy peach dress for one of her weddings. "When Marie's family offered to give her a wedding outfit, she asked them to buy her a dark dress that she could wear to her lab the next day."

"Well, her marriage lasted longer than any of mine," Elaine had said, "so maybe there's something to that." I couldn't have said it better myself.

With Elaine on the phone now, I took the opportunity to talk about Margaret Hurley's death and my idea that it might not have been accidental. I brought up the tricky helium vote and what I knew about Cavallo's report. Cavallo worked at the lab on Charger Street in Revere, the same one that had a lot to do with why my left arm was sore, and how I'd come to know Matt so well.

"I was only kidding when I asked about new murders," Elaine said. "You're really getting into this homicide business. This is not the Gloria I know. I can't picture it."

"Maybe you should come for a visit and see for yourself."

"I don't know. I think I'll wait till you have a real apartment. I was a little freaked out by your living situation. Is this congresswoman's body going to be waked in your house, too?"

I drew in my breath at the reminder of where I lived. I carried my cordless phone to my rocker where I'd left the *Globe* and scanned to the end of the article. I let out a near whistle, and Elaine knew the answer to her question.

"She's going to be right there in your living room, isn't she?" Elaine said, mimicking the voice of the narrator of a scary radio show.

"Not exactly in my living room," I said, straightening up as if Elaine could see my defensive posture. "On the first floor of the building I live in."

Although I was getting used to having my home address constantly in the obituary column of local newspapers, I renewed my determination to look for an apartment in a real building, one with no noises from an embalming prep room or stacks of funeral-car stickers and prayer cards on a table in my foyer. I wasn't about to give in to Elaine, however.

"I like this apartment," I said. "It's light and comfortable, and I'm settled in. You know how I hate to move."

"Right." Elaine laughed. "You only go for dramatic moves—leave your hometown when you're twenty-two and don't go back, not even for a visit. You stay in the same place for thirty-three years, then leave and return to your hometown. Doesn't everybody do that?"

After Elaine's call, I wandered around my apartment, unable to focus my attention on a single task. I took out my notes for the presentation I had to give in a week for my friend Peter Mastrone's Italian class. After an unsuccessful attempt to renew our high-school romance, Peter and I were now working on an unsuccessful friendship. Peter had been unhappy about my work with Matt from the beginning, and except for the commitment I'd made to visit his classroom once a month, I would have enforced a no-contact rule.

Fortunately, I loved the interaction with Peter's students and looked forward to the next visit, timed to coincide with the anniversary of Marconi's invention of the radio—December 12, 1901. The overall theme of my talks was the contribution of Italians and Italian-Americans to science and technology. I gave the talks in English, but the students wrote their reports in Italian, thus helping me brush up on the language of my parents at the same time. There hadn't been many Lamerinos, Galiganis, or Gennaros in my blond California neighborhood. People whose names did end in a vowel were more likely to celebrate El Cinco de

Mayo, Mexican Independence Day, than Columbus Day.

After a brief review of Marconi's wireless system and the first message transmitted across the Atlantic, I put down my notes and renewed my wandering. Thanks to Josephine's neatness gene, even in my idleness I accomplished something, picking up a crumb here, a stray piece of paper there, straightening a pile of newspapers. My version of good housekeeping was much less compulsive than Josephine's, however; I couldn't claim as she did that "you can eat off my floors."

Each time I passed my phone, I had a strong urge to call Matt. I had no such urge to use my exercise bicycle, situated at the foot of my bed, like a legless soldier with arms open to capture me.

I reminded myself that I'd see Matt at dinner with Rose and Frank in a couple of hours. I still wasn't comfortable calling Matt "for no reason," or just because I couldn't wait to compare notes on an item in the news.

I walked to my window and studied my favorite scene—the Romanesque tower of St. Anthony's Church outlined against a dull gray sky, streaked with a tiny remnant of sunset red. We'd had an early storm over the weekend, and the trees were heavy with snow. I mentally renewed my minority position that a murky East Coast sky was more soothing than the stark bright sun of the Pacific.

Rose and Frank saved me from further daydreaming by coming upstairs after closing their offices on the floors below me. We'd planned to ride together to Anzoni's restaurant and meet Matt there.

"Then he can drive you home," Rose had said, "and, you know, you can invite him up." Rose was convinced that I didn't know the first thing about dating, and she wasn't shy about giving me advice.

"Just met what's left of the Hurley family," Frank said, entering my living room. He plucked a tiny piece of lint from his perfectly pressed jacket. *The Galiganis are the lint police,* I thought, and I pictured their closets beating out an industrial laboratory, meeting all the government requirements for a class-A clean room.

"That brother is something else," Frank said. "Now I remember the stories of his gambling, and how the grandmother cut him out of her will."

"Tell me more," I said, trying to sound casual, while at the same time avoiding a disapproving look from Rose.

"Frank," was all she said, and Frank went silent.

I guessed she was using a certain pitch that Frank recognized as the director's sign for "cut."

"Rose," I whined, "you know I can keep a confidence."

"And you know that's not why I'm cutting this off. I know you, Gloria. You're just looking for an excuse to call this a murder. That bullet didn't teach you anything, did it?"

"Frank," I begged, "what exactly was Buddy's demeanor?"

Rose and Frank roared with laughter and even I

couldn't believe what had happened to my vocabulary. "Now I know you've gone off the edge, Gloria," Rose said. "You sound like Court TV."

I had to admit she had a point.

Chapter Three

Most of the changes I'd come back to in Revere were for the better, with the grand exception of the Boulevard. Once famous for its beach and boardwalk, Revere's Boulevard had been lined with roller coasters and Ferris wheels, carousels, hot dog vendors, and frozen custard stands. My first pay envelope, with fifty cents for every hour I'd worked, came from my skilled labor at Johnny's Cotton Candy Counter.

The Boulevard now held multilevel condominium complexes, liberally sprinkled with miniparks of a few benches and trees. All of the rides and, with only a couple of exceptions, all of the food concessions of the first public beach in the United States had been leveled to the ground one way or another.

Anzoni's new restaurant was on the site of the old Tilt-A-Whirl. If it weren't for my overwhelming sadness at the loss of the entire two-mile strip of amusements, I would have considered a good Italian restaurant an improvement over a thrill ride. I'd worked behind counters on the Boulevard all through my years at Revere High School, but never once rode anything more risky than a bumper car. My guess is that Josephine told me I'd be scared.

As soon as we pulled up in back of Anzoni's, just after seven o'clock, I saw Matt's steel blue Camry. I felt the now familiar twinge in my chest and paused only a fraction of a second before acknowledging that it was not due only to the thirty-degree air that greeted us outside the car.

Matt stood up as we entered, hitting a faux Italian olive tree, and catching the few strands of hair that covered the top of his head in its leaves. Anzoni's was done up in deep burgundies with faux Tiffany lamps and faux sculptures. Only the food and the tiny poinsettia plants on the tables were authentic.

Matt caught my eye and smiled.

"Gloria," he said, nodding. "Rose. Frank."

His smile was warm, his voice comfortably deep, but from his clipped tone, you might have thought we were preparing for a lineup. Matt had been widowed for many years and, by his own account, had given all his attention to his job. He was as awkward as I was in social situations. One of his charms, I thought.

Matt ran his hand along his dark blue tie, tucking it into his brown suit jacket. As usual, he took my coat, a long lapis lazuli blue that Rose had talked me into. I'd held my ground on jewelry, however, and wore a small hand-painted set of wooden bells instead of the elaborate holiday pin Rose suggested.

I had mixed feelings about Matt's chivalry, of course, since I'd lived my life in a man's profession and without a partner. I'd never allowed any deference to my gender in the laboratory, but when Matt pulled out a chair or held the door for me, it was a different story. I resolved to research the latest feminist thinking on male/female etiquette.

We settled around the small square table, juggling hats and gloves and scarves—another difference between the coasts. In California I kept my winter clothes with my luggage since I needed them only on business trips to cold climates. I'd forgotten what it was like to need an extra chair for woolens.

"How are your classes, Gloria?" Matt asked. He knew about my series for Peter as well as a science education project I was finishing up for a school in San Francisco, and always acted interested—something else I liked about him.

"I'm ready for Marconi," I said, picking up a napkin. "Shall I draw you a picture?"

"Oh, no," said Rose as she snatched the cloth from my hand and told Matt how that was my trademark—using restaurant napkins as a chalkboard for unsolicited science lessons.

"Just kidding," I said, placing the linen across my lap. "I'd never deface a cloth napkin."

I wondered how long it would be before Matt and I had our own stories. We'd only been seeing each other socially for a few weeks, five to be exact. Two jazz concerts, one movie, and four dinners, two of them alone, to be even more exact. Each event had ended with affectionate, huglike contact, such as I exchanged with my cousin Mary Ann in Worcester at the beginning and end of our infrequent visits. So far, that was enough for me. I hadn't experienced more physical intimacy than that since my late fiancé, Al, and I practiced "safe necking" many years ago.

By the time my three present-day companions and I had finished an antipasto and four orders of Anzoni's special, eggplant parmigiana, we'd covered all the neutral topics—holiday shopping, the stock market, and the doings of the three Galigani children. Rose was especially proud that their middle child, John, who was the editor of the *Revere Journal*, had just won an award for best regional reporting in Suffolk County.

Frank told us about his week at a convention in Houston, sponsored by funeral home suppliers. He described the exhibits, but it didn't take long to exhaust the subject of caskets and vaults, at least at the level appropriate for dinner conversation.

Finally, I plunged in.

"How about that Hurley case," I said to no one and everyone, including the young waiter in a short white jacket who was setting down our cappuccinos, as if the question couldn't be more casual. My voice had risen in pitch, however, like the whistle of an oncoming train, and I knew I was fooling no one.

Each of my dinner companions turned to me, heads slightly tilted, looking like a poorly orchestrated puppet show. Even *I* tilted my head, as if the mouth that uttered those words didn't really belong to me.

"It certainly is a great loss," said Frank, the first to recover. He was, after all, trained as a bereavement counselor. "Margaret Hurley was doing an excellent job for us."

Usually I could tell when Frank was in his funeral director mode, but this time I couldn't guess whether he actually knew how Hurley was performing in Congress or if he pulled the line from his undertaker script. I was a little off-balance from Anzoni's low-level lighting and the tightness in my throat as I tried to read Matt's expression.

"A great loss," Matt said, and put down his cup. "As a matter of fact, Gloria, I'd like to talk to you about working with us on a limited basis. The congresswoman's briefcase was full of technical papers and notes and we'd like to understand a little more what they are. Not that we think the material had anything to do with the incident; it's just for completeness."

It was hard to hear myself over the sighs of Rose and Frank, but I managed a weak, "I could come by tomorrow morning?"

My brain was swimming with messages. From Matt I sifted out "limited basis," as opposed to "whole hog," which more aptly described my involvement in the last case I'd worked on. Rose's deep intake of breath carried the worry that I'd be in danger again, and Frank's outtake expressed relief that no protocol had been breached.

What I wasn't prepared for was Matt's next comment.

"If you'll excuse me," he said, "I have to be going. About ten tomorrow morning, Gloria?" He'd already taken out his wallet and slid several bills over to Frank.

So much for Rose's plan, I thought.

"Ten is fine," I said.

The ride back to Galigani's Mortuary and my home seemed as long as the wait for a calculation from the computer I'd used in graduate school in the 1960s. Rose chattered about how well their older son Robert managed the business on his own while Frank was in Houston, and how Mary Catherine, their youngest and my godchild, was getting used to her new job as a chemical engineer for an oil company.

I mentioned that I had a lot of reading to do for Peter's class next week. I stressed the time-consuming tasks of preparing student handouts and transparencies, and compiling virtually tons of reference material, as if I didn't have a minute to spare for the likes of Matt Gennaro.

I'd never been able to break the habit of replaying scenes in my past, especially those that seemed to go wrong, and the scene at Anzoni's, with Matt's unexpected leaving, was no exception. I went over every nuance, and thought of three or four alternatives for every word I'd used. *If I'd been this careful reviewing my physics research,* I thought, *I'd probably have won the Nobel Prize.*

What didn't fit together were Matt's invitation to work with him, indicating that my Hurley question wasn't totally out of line, and his abrupt departure. Usually—meaning the two other times the four of us had met for dinner—Matt drove me home and came upstairs for coffee.

During those visits, we'd reminisced about the old Revere Beach, and the big stars that had performed at the Wonderland Ballroom and other clubs on the Boardwalk—crooners like Jerry Vale and Freddie Cannon, Liberace, and a very young Barbra Streisand, to name a few.

Matt and I had explored each other's interests, doing spontaneous film reviews and book reports, although neither one of us was a big fan of movies or fiction. I'd learned to enjoy abstruse foreign films in Berkeley, but not enough to find out where they played in the Boston area.

Matt watched only "Star Trek" and read only Tom Clancy and I stayed with one or two classics a year. We'd both poured more energy into conferences and professional journals. I was amazed to discover that Matt had to do as much as any physicist to keep up with the latest in his field, from new weapons on the street to advances in crime detection techniques. And I'd certainly never heard of the periodicals Matt read, like *Forensics Today* and *The American Detective*.

I realized how much I'd looked forward to a similar end to this evening, and felt a wave of disappointment that seemed to fold my shoulders into the posture of a dying swan. As usual, I focused on the negative, almost forgetting that Matt had invited me to work with him again, which was what I'd hoped for from the moment I'd read the Hurley headlines. More credit to Josephine, I thought, who taught me by example to give any negative an order of magnitude more weight than a positive.

I wanted to hop out of the car, to the extent that someone of my size-fourteen frame can hop, and hide in my comfortable bedroom with a box of See's candy and a disc of Pachelbel's *Canon*. I remembered, however, that I was on the wrong coast for See's and I didn't own the *Canon*. I'd started to redesign my self-pity scenario, when Rose and Frank interrupted.

"Mind if we come up?" Rose asked.

"I really think I'm ready for bed," I said, giving her the girlfriend-to-girlfriend look that begged for understanding.

"Actually, I have to check something in the files," Frank said. "It'll only take a minute."

Before I could say anything else, we were all out of the car, trudging up the Tuttle St. driveway against the cold wind that had come up from the ocean, less than a mile away. I loved the smell of the salt air right at my fingertips, or at least my windowsill, and it no longer bothered me that the trip to my front door included walking past a large but tasteful sign that advertised the presence of a mortuary chapel, with full funeral services.

As we entered the lobby, I noticed the menu-type bulletin board already in place in front of the larger of Galigani's two first-floor parlors:

MARGARET MARY HURLEY
7:00 P.M. to 9:00 P.M.
Rosary 8:00 P.M.

"Is the body here now?" I asked. I wanted no surprises, like a garage door opening in the middle of the night to admit a hearse.

"There has been no release to us yet," Frank answered. I could always count on Frank's language to be smooth and bloodless, disguising the real nature of his "clients," as he referred to them. An eavesdropper this evening might think we were talking about the release of new government data or a pop music album.

Frank stopped at his office, at the back of the first floor, and Rose came up two more flights to my apartment. She headed for my kitchen and started water for tea, mumbling as usual about my meager larder of food and drink. I thought I was doing well to have coffee, several varieties of herbal tea, and cookies from the gourmet section of the supermarket. We both wished we'd taken home orders of Anzoni's tiramisu or tartufo. I blamed Matt for distracting us by his untimely exit.

The water was hardly boiling when Frank came in, with a wide grin on his face.

"I was right," he said, "but I wanted to be sure. I thought I remembered that it was around the holidays that Matt's wife died. Sure enough, I checked the file, and it was December fifth, nineteen eighty-six. That's ten years ago today."

Frank looked at me, standing straight, palms up, as

if he'd just finished a brilliant summary in a courtroom trial.

"Thanks, Frank," I said, my long sigh in harmony with Rose's.

Chapter Four

As predicted, a light snow was falling on Tuesday morning, mounting in even piles on my east-facing windowsills. I turned on my TV and heard the weatherperson say that the snowfall for November and December had exceeded amounts in previous years. I felt it was my own private welcome home. Especially now that I didn't have to shovel my own driveway, or commute to work every day, snow seemed even more romantically beautiful than I remembered.

TV clips of Margaret Hurley featured her youth in Revere and Boston, her relationship with Frances Whitestone, and her short career in Congress. I was a little embarrassed at myself for grabbing a notebook when the announcer turned to her personal life and hinted at her brother's shady deals and her stormy parting with her fiancé, Patrick Gallagher, also of Revere. And, to add a little spice, listeners were reminded of how Margaret had publicly denounced both men, at different times, for different reasons. So much for speaking ill of the dead, I thought.

I'd forgotten to check my answering machine after Anzoni's, so I had to drink my breakfast coffee to the sound of Peter Mastrone's voice.

"Just a reminder that your talk is next Monday. I've missed seeing you, Gloria. Turns out that Monday is a half-day for us, so maybe we can have lunch after class. It's been a while."

In fact, it had been a couple of weeks since I'd seen Peter, but what was that compared to the thirty-odd years we hadn't been in touch at all? Rose claimed that Peter kept up with her and Frank just to keep track of me, and I was beginning to think she was right. If so, it didn't say much for the choices Peter had made in life.

I decided that instead of returning his phone call, I'd work on his class. But not until I'd brushed up on helium. I had no intention of meeting Matt Gennaro unprepared. Especially if his partner, George Berger, was in the office. I'd managed to get along with Berger during my previous contract only because he was out most of the time helping with his new baby. The child was a couple of months old by now, so I could hardly hope that he'd still be on paternity leave.

Berger had made no secret of his dislike and distrust of me. He probably wouldn't have made as much fuss if the department had given a contract to a tarot-card reader. The first time we met he listed his own credentials in science: several classes at Revere High

School, plus college chemistry, plus forensic chemistry when he trained as a detective. I put him somewhere above *Reader's Digest*, but below *Scientific American*, though I didn't tell him that. I could hardly wait to see how we'd work together this time, if we had to.

To brighten my mood, I put on a disc of Christmas music, a medley of old favorites by Perry Como. I pulled out my "interesting articles" folder and took it with my mug of coffee to my new, cushy, blue-gray corduroy couch. Relocating three thousand miles away had given me an excellent excuse to buy new furniture. I'd ended up keeping only my two favorite rockers, plus anything that plugged in. As a technology junkie, I got attached to computers and stereo equipment, but hardly ever to wood or fabric. I wondered if Perry Como had a PC.

I sorted through the wide accordion folder and located several clippings on the helium reserves.

One name that kept coming up was that of William Carey, the CEO of CompTech, a software company based in Texas and specializing in database management. The company also had a branch office and a small distribution plant in Chelsea, one town away from Revere.

One article reported on Carey's appearance at a Congressional hearing on the helium-storage program. In his prepared remarks, Carey had stressed the need for the government's maintaining control over enough helium to guarantee our predominance in future technologies. Why did a software company care so much about helium? I wondered.

As I looked through my own stockpile of helium literature, I realized that the political maneuverings were far more complicated than the physical principles underlying the accumulation of helium. As difficult as it was to mine helium, it seemed easier than distilling the truth about the program from vested-interest doublespeak.

No two articles agreed on how long the helium supply would last. Factoring out all the differences in the way the calculations were made, I concluded that the best estimates were: about ten years for worldwide use, and close to one hundred years if limited to federal government use.

It was even more difficult to figure out the budget for the program—did it cost only two million dollars a year as one group suggested, or was it 1.2 billion dollars in debt as another claimed?

I'd had success in the past when I prepared lists and charts for Matt, so I decided to do that again, starting with the simple part, the science. I made a list of facts about helium that made it a special commodity, and desirable to have on hand:

- Helium occurs naturally in small amounts in natural gas deposits.
- It must be extracted and stored as soon as the gas is mined, or it escapes into the atmosphere and can't be reclaimed for useful purposes.

- No other element can reach the low temperature of liquid helium.
- This low temperature is required for many emerging technologies.
- Demand for helium is rising about ten percent a year.

There was a lot more I could go into—details about how the federal government got involved in the first place, for example, since private companies also mine and sell helium. For the moment, I decided I'd done enough. For all I knew, this science lesson was far off the mark and I'd wasted my time.

At nine o'clock I dropped my notes into my brief-case and headed for the closet to choose a light-snowfall outfit. Since this was my first New England winter in a while, my cold-weather wardrobe choices were limited. I did have one pair of black knee-length boots, suitable for walking through slush, so I built around them, choosing a wide black skirt with silvery threads and a gray cowl-neck sweater—uninspired, but at least warm and coordinated.

I poked around in my box of scatter pins, sustaining only minor stab wounds, and came up with a neutral holiday design, an abstract ceramic sleigh that I'd picked up at a crafts fair in Berkeley. I wasn't sure about Berger's religious connections, if any, and didn't want to annoy him any more than I already did by my presence. Surely the father of a newborn couldn't take offense at the suggestion of Santa's vehicle.

As for my own vehicle choices, I'd finally gotten rid of the Jeep I'd driven from California, so my only source of transportation now was the shiny black Cadillac I'd bought from the Galiganis. I still couldn't bring myself to say "my Cadillac," but there it was, and it got me safely to Matt's office at the Revere Police Department on Pleasant Street.

I entered the old building and identified myself to the uniformed officer sitting behind a thick pane of glass, which I supposed to be bulletproof. Except that it was no larger than a few square feet, the foyer, painted in a bright blue, looked more like the box office for a theater than the stepping-stone to law enforcement.

As I approached Matt's office, I could see Berger's short, stocky frame through the frosted-glass window. He stood with his back to the door, facing Matt. I threw my shoulders back, shifted my briefcase to my left hand, and entered the office, ready for battle.

With only the briefest nod to Matt, I launched into my offense.

"Sgt. Berger," I said, "I hope you have pictures to show me."

Berger's eyebrows went up into the shape of a question mark just briefly, then he reached into his jacket and brought out a yellow envelope full of Kodak moments.

I saw a wide grin come over his face and knew that my strategy had worked, at least for the moment. As I shuffled through the photos, I made noises of admiration, wishing I knew the gender of the child. After counting no fewer than six different shades of pink in the clothing and general environment of the baby, I used my skills as a physicist/detective and took a risk.

"She's beautiful," I said.

"Her name's Cynthia," Berger said, still grinning.

"Beautiful," I said again, and actually meant it. I was a traditionalist when it came to names, making fun of the new trends and the unlikely cultural combinations. In a class I taught in San Francisco one semester, I had two young men named Ian Wong. Not that I was against interracial marriage, just interracial names.

If I had children, I thought, I'd probably number them until they were old enough to choose for themselves—too much responsibility to give a lifetime label to a person. Another advantage I'd noticed in moving back to Revere was that people here, at least the old-timers, could spell and pronounce my name without trouble.

" 'Cynthia Berger' has the ring of a cellist at Carnegie Hall or a Nobelist in literature," I said, happy to be flattering and honest at the same time. "You must be really proud."

"We are," Berger said. What I saw in the vicinity of Matt's eyes came very close to a wink.

I took a seat and Berger excused himself to go to a meeting. As he left the office he shook my hand and said, "I told Matt you were the one to help us with this. Most of it is pretty straightforward, and I could handle it, but there are a couple of things I think you could clear up.''

I sat facing Matt across his desk and we both sighed the equivalent of ''whew.''

''I think fatherhood agrees with him,'' I said.

Matt shook his head. ''Maybe,'' he said, ''but your fancy footwork didn't hurt. Nice work, Gloria.''

Matt was always generous with his compliments, but not so free that I doubted his sincerity. Just the right level for a woman of my generation who had a hard time accepting praise for anything but her spaghetti.

''Before we get into this,'' Matt said, lifting a folder from the pile on his neat desk, ''I wanted to say something about last night.''

''You don't have to.''

''I know that, but I want to. It was a difficult day for me and I probably shouldn't have made dinner plans in the first place.''

I debated with myself about mentioning that I knew of the anniversary, worried that Matt had an entirely different reason for leaving without me, so to speak.

''Yesterday was the tenth anniversary of Teresa's death,'' Matt said, removing my dilemma. ''Sometimes I forget and other times . . .''

''I know. Frank told me. I'm sorry. And I suppose we never really forget completely.''

''That's right,'' Matt said. ''In my own world here, I forgot about Al.''

Matt and I had talked a little about the circumstances of the death of my late fiancé, Al Gravese.

Matt had just joined the police force at the time and remembered the rumors of foul play. I wondered if this were a good time to tell him that I intended to do some research on Al's business connections and the car crash that killed him, and that I could use his help. I looked at him, still appearing vulnerable, and decided not to.

"I knew Al only a short time compared to you and Teresa," I said.

"Thanks for understanding, Gloria," he said. "Maybe we can make it up this weekend?"

"You have nothing to make up," I said. "But I do happen to have some time this weekend." If I were filling out one of the dozens of questionnaires that I'd seen in my lifetime, I would have called myself "extremely satisfied."

Matt turned to his desk and I knew that personal talk was over and it was time for business. He had a way of shifting abruptly from one to the other with the speed of a bullet. He handed me a manila folder thick with papers.

"Here are some of the documents we found in Ms. Hurley's briefcase," he said, holding up one of the widest attaché cases I'd ever seen. "They probably have nothing to do with this hit-and-run, but it bothers me to have papers in my file that I can't understand. Why don't you get a start on these while I dig out a contract. And if you can hold off on coffee for the moment, maybe we can catch an early lunch with the real thing at Russo's?"

I gave a grateful nod and watched him as he left

the office, until he rounded a corner. I thought how lucky I was to have met him and, with a nod to Josephine, questioned whether I deserved him.

I put the folder on my lap and opened it. The first document was printed on bright blue shadow-print letterhead—*CompTech, Inc., William E. Carey, President and Chief Executive Officer.*

Chapter Five

Matt's side of the room was almost completely without decoration. The only photo on his desk was one of his parents at an anniversary celebration. A bulletin board behind his desk held a haphazard arrangement of memos, lists, and telephone messages on small yellow slips of paper. I wondered if Rose would consider a framed fine-arts poster a personal enough Christmas gift.

By the time Matt returned, I'd gone through at least two inches of documents, many of them contracts between CompTech and the various government agencies charged with maintaining the helium operations, principally the Bureau of Mines and the Department of the Interior.

I thought it was strange that a facility that Congress was about to close would still be awarding multimillion-dollar contracts for services such as computer upgrades and training for its more than two hundred employees. I wondered if Congresswoman Hurley thought it was strange, too. Why else was she carrying this material around during her Christmas vacation?

Matt presented me with my contract, a simple two-pager, looking even more straightforward than I remembered, next to the legal jungle I'd just been struggling through.

"Will it do any good for me to remind you of your limited duties?" Matt asked. "No work on your own; you're not an officer of the city, and so on?"

"Is this like reading me my rights?"

"This time you may not even have to leave this office. I just want some intelligent notes on the technical contents of Ms. Hurley's papers."

"I'll need to take copies of these technical papers with me," I said. "I'll write out a summary of each one and we can go from there."

"Sounds good."

"Is this everything you have?" I asked, gesturing toward the large brown briefcase dominating the small space between Matt's desk and the wall.

"That's everything," he said.

"While you were out, I looked at these contracts with CompTech," I said, thumbing the edge of the sheaf of papers as if it were a flip book. "I knew that the CEO, William Carey, has been giving testimony in favor of keeping the helium facility going. Now I see why—the operation has been his bread and butter for several years. Suppose Hurley were going to vote to close it. He might have been desperate enough to . . .''

Matt stood up, both palms up like a stop signal for a jumbo jet at Logan Airport. He shook his head and came out with the laugh I liked best, the one that sounded like ''whoa.''

''Why am I not surprised?'' he asked.

''Now that we've opened the subject,'' I said, ''Frank mentioned that Hurley's brother, Brendan, is a heavy gambler and was cut out of his father's will. Evidently he blames Margaret and has been trying to contest it for the past ten years.''

There must be something about Matt's office, I thought, *that releases my inhibitions and turns me into the assertive woman that I'm just getting to know.* For better or worse, it didn't carry over into our personal relationship, but I took advantage of the feeling of the moment.

''It just doesn't seem likely that a car would be driving full speed ahead like that down Oxford Park, fast enough to ram into someone and kill her. It's practically a cul-de-sac. The only thing you can do at the end of that street is circle around and come back on Revere Street or dead-end at Folsom.''

''I know,'' Matt said. ''I know. And that's why we're not ruling out a deliberate attack. But that doesn't mean you should be involved. This was a politician, not a scientist.''

''Except for this.'' I waved the papers in the air again, moving in on the little opening Matt had given me. I found myself remembering all the times I'd heard that on courtroom TV dramas—"he's opened the door on that," they'd say. *I must really be lowering my standards,* I thought, *if I'm taking my cues from prime-time television.*

"Hurley was on the Science and Technology Committee and about to vote on something with very high stakes," I said to Matt, shaking my head a bit to get rid of the images of actors in my head. "I'm just saying that I'll keep that in mind as I read these papers."

I gave him a "not to worry" smile and heard what I took to be a sigh of resignation. I knew that Matt worried about my safety, so I was all the more pleased that he would trust me to work on this case in the first place. I hadn't exactly behaved myself the last time.

Matt looked at his watch. "Do you have anything to do around town for now?" he asked. "I have a few things to take care of, then I'll meet you at Russo's at eleven-thirty."

"That'll be fine," I said. "Maybe I'll go to the library and start my limited duties."

I'm not sure I ever had any intention of going to the library, but I ended up only a few doors away from the police station, at the office of the *Revere Journal,* the city's primary newspaper. I told myself that it was too cold to walk all the way down Pleasant Street and over to Beach where the library was. The digital display on the bank across the street supported my reasoning—it was ten-thirty in the morning and twenty-nine degrees.

John Galigani, Rose and Frank's second son, had

been editor of the newspaper for about three years. The receptionist called back to him and less than ten minutes after leaving Matt's office, I'd been set up in the *Journal*'s musty, little-used basement with microfiche files for the year 1962. It wasn't a coincidence that I had Al's notebook with me, though I wasn't exactly certain how I would use it.

"No problem, Gloria," John had said, tossing back his extra-long brown hair, a source of contention between him and his perfectly groomed father. John had rubbed his hands together when I told him what I needed, as if this would be the easiest thing he'd do all day. All of Rose and Frank's children treated me like royalty, confirming my view that other people's offspring are much better companions for me than my own would have been.

I inserted a blue plastic card into the microfiche reader and breathed in deeply, acquiring an uncomfortable dose of dust. I wrinkled my nose and scrolled to December.

Al's crash had been on the Friday before Christmas, December 21, 1962. He'd canceled a date with me that evening, telling me he had "business." It wasn't unusual for that to happen, and I never knew the nature of the business. I remember actually being thrilled by his secret life, as if that gave me status. Josephine was already dead when I met Al, who was working at the Zarelli Nursery, owned by Rose's family. I was so proud of the way he lavished gifts on me and my father, peeling off bills from the roll he always carried.

''Here, Marco,'' he'd say to my father, ''go play some horses.''

''Al's a nice boy,'' my father would say, and I'd be relieved that finally I'd pleased at least one of my parents.

How was it that I never wondered how a thirty-year-old landscaper managed to accumulate thick wads of fifties? I could now understand how Diane Keaton's character, Kay, was fooled for a while by her God-father husband, even as she saw lines of men waiting to kiss his hand.

Over the years I'd forgiven myself for my enormous lapse of judgment. I chalked it up to the times, to my youth, and to my incredible need to be wanted by someone who seemed important.

With less than an hour to work before meeting Matt at Russo's, the most I could do was locate the articles about the car crash and print them out. The reports on the inquiry into the crash ran into early February 1963, then petered out. I had hardly any memory of reading the news or seeing the grainy crash-scene photos the first time they were printed. I didn't leave the area until three months after the crash, but it made sense that I'd avoided the media coverage at the time.

The notebook I'd carried with me to the *Journal* office was the one I'd found in the attic a few months ago, its brittle yellowed pages filled with names and numbers and dollar signs. The next step in my plan was to see if those names were in the news for any reason around the time of the crash. What I really hoped for was Matt's help to give me access to the police files for that time, but that opportunity hadn't quite gelled.

I packed up my slippery copies from the microfiche printer and headed for Russo's, another in the long list of Revere restaurants with phony Italian decor, but genuinely delicious Italian food.

Tuesday was blue suit day for Matt, I'd figured out, and as I sat across from him I tried to remember if I'd ever seen the tie he was wearing, a maroon paisley. I'd been counting his ties—an embarrassing occupational hazard. I always felt I had a good handle on things when I had an accurate count of some variable.

We ordered chicken pesto sandwiches and cappuccinos and got down to business before the food arrived. I tried to cover the fact that I hadn't done any homework since I left him.

"I've made a few notes about the helium program," I said, pulling out the charts and lists I'd made the night before. I went over the fact sheet about how helium is extracted, then added some details about the federal operation.

"The Bureau of Mines owns and operates an extraction and purification plant, plus peripheral facilities," I said, "in Amarillo, Texas, not far from the main headquarters of Carey's company. I haven't looked over these contracts carefully yet, but I see two possible reasons why Carey would be unhappy with the congresswoman. One, she might be a deciding vote to kill the program, or two, she might have found out that these contracts were way out of line for a program with a questionable future.''

''Tell me again why the government is involved in the first place?''

Matt had chosen not to respond to my brilliant analysis of motive for murder, so I stayed on his topic.

''It started with the Helium Act of 1960. The Bureau of Mines was supposed to buy and sell helium without loss to taxpayers and also make sure that we'd have enough for emerging technologies, independent of what private industry was doing.''

''And these emerging technologies are?''

I was used to Matt's style by now, and enjoyed filling in the blanks at the ends of his sentences.

''Computers, low-temperature medical applications, high-speed transportation systems, high-purity manufacturing. The trouble is the plan didn't work. The operation is in debt and that's why most reps in Congress want to shut it down.''

Matt's beeper went off, as if to signal the end of class. We'd finished our lunch, and I had about run out of information, so the timing was good.

''Give me a call when you've gone through the papers,'' Matt said.

We'd already started out Russo's door, and stepped onto Broadway. The aromas of garlic and espresso couldn't compete with the weather, so within a few seconds all I could smell was dry, freezing air. We clutched the tops of our coats and bent our heads against the wind.

"I'm sure I'll have it finished by the time I see you at the wake tomorrow evening," I said.

"Do you attend the wake for everyone laid out at Galigani's?" Matt asked.

"No, but this one is sure to draw a lot more people than usual," I said. "Probably hundreds, from all over the district and beyond."

"So?" Matt said.

"So, I told Rose and Frank I'd help them out."

I focused my eyes downward, as if putting on my gloves required all my attention, and started to list things I might help with, like taking care of Father Tucci when he came to lead the rosary, and being sure the guest books were in place, but I didn't get very far before Matt started his laugh.

I waited for the "whoa," then joined him.

Chapter Six

I drove home with more-than-usual attention to the road, which was still icy from the last storm. As a result, I didn't start making my mental list until I pulled into the mortuary garage and parked alongside the hearse. Its neat white chintz curtains on the back and side windows gave it the look of a Harvard Square café, but I knew better.

My list began with my assignment from Matt, then my class for Peter, and, least interesting of all, Christmas shopping. The only purchases I'd made while shopping with Rose were some ornaments and Christmas linens that I hadn't even removed from the bags yet.

No one on my Christmas list was easy to buy for. Thinking of Rose and Frank's beautiful home on the other side of town, and their magnificent wardrobes, I was stuck before I started. Elaine Cody had a closet full of equally elegant clothing, and a lovely old house in Berkeley, furnished with heirlooms and antiques.

I'll buy everyone books, I thought, *just like every other year.*

I entered the main foyer of the building from the garage, which put me under the stairway to the upper floors.

Even before I reached the first step, I heard voices from the main parlor, where Margaret Hurley was to be waked. I couldn't resist the temptation to investigate, and wondered when I'd become so nosy.

Fortunately for my reputation, should anyone care, I had the excuse that I was looking for mail on the table by the door. No one had to know that Martha, Rose's assistant, took my mail up to my apartment every day, and left it in front of my door. What I was looking through were flyers about the services offered by Galigani's Mortuary.

I sneaked a glance into the main parlor and saw Robert Galigani talking to a tall man with red hair and clenched fists. He was wearing a serious winter jacket, the kind Californians used only for ski trips.

"I'm her fiancé," I heard him say, relaxing his fingers long enough to point a finger at Robert.

I hadn't seen Robert in action before, and I was impressed that he'd adopted his father's easy, calm style.

"I'm sorry, Mr. Gallagher," Robert said, "but I'm sure you know that Mrs. Whitestone is Ms. Hurley's executor, and in charge of the arrangements. And according to her, you two have been estranged for some

time. Mrs. Whitestone has asked that you not be included in the special visitations. I'm afraid we're
bound to follow Mrs. Whitestone's directives.''

"So I can't even see her?''

"You'll be very welcome here, during regular visiting hours, I can assure you of that. For now, I can
offer you a cup of coffee back in my office.''

"That will be the day I'll come when the old lady's
here. She never liked me. She was worse than a
mother-in-law would have been.''

He turned to leave, and I caught a glimpse of his
very red face before I turned and left myself. As I
climbed the stairs to my apartment, I had no trouble
picturing Mr. Gallagher ramming his car into his ex-
fiancé.

I'd hardly gotten started on my assignments when I
found myself in the middle of a meeting in my living
room.

"That's why we hired Martha, and Tony, and Sal,''
Rose said. "To help out at times like this. So we don't
have to use our friends.''

"She just wants to be near the action,'' Frank said.

"I know that, and that's what I don't want,'' Rose
answered, folding her arms across her chest and shifting her body away from Frank. The two of them managed to look uncomfortable on my soft, wide-wale
corduroy couch, while I sat across from them on my
glide rocker.

The only thing that could make this worse, I
thought, *would be if Peter Mastrone were here also.*

Peter had expressed great displeasure at my new career. At least Rose's nagging was from her genuine concern for me. Peter's, I felt, stemmed from his desire to control me, as if our thirty-odd-year separation was but a long weekend.

"What's the big deal?" Robert asked, from the matching rocker on my right. Knowing that his parents were in my apartment, Robert had made an innocent trip upstairs to visit. He probably wanted a cup of coffee and a simple chat, I thought, and not this imbroglio over my volunteerism.

I'd been watching them and listening to the three of them discuss me as if I were an employee applicant, sitting miles away. I decided to enter the debate, with only a slight exaggeration of the truth.

"Matt didn't think it was a problem," I said. "I'll just wander around, checking on things, and be as inconspicuous as possible."

"What things?" Rose asked. "You'll be cross-examining and asking for alibis."

"Cool," Robert said, sounding like his fourteen-year-old son, and the Galigani's only grandchild. Rose shot him a look that would have sent him to his room in his preteen years.

"And what were you looking for in the *Journal*'s morgue anyway?" Rose asked me.

So that's it, I thought. *John squealed.*

"Are you looking into Al's crash?" Frank asked. I was grateful that he tried to sound matter-of-fact, as if it were normal for someone to split town when her fiancé dies, then come back three decades later to investigate.

I lifted my chin in an act of self-confidence and caught a glimpse of my San Francisco poster on the wall opposite my rockers. The cable car in the print appeared to wobble around its perch at the top of a steep hill.

"I'm perfectly capable of taking care of myself," I said, turning away from the image of the gravity-defying trolley. "I'm working on this case now, and I need to get to know the people involved."

Frank slapped his knees and stood up.

"Why don't we have some coffee and make a little plan that makes everyone happy? Luberto's can have cannoli here in fifteen minutes."

Frank picked up the phone and pushed Luberto's number, apparently from memory. *He doesn't go to seminars for nothing*, I thought. And, trim and fit as he was, Frank used the time-tested method of easing tension—food and drink.

"I'll grind some fresh Vienna roast," I said, "and I even stopped at Happy Farms today. There's fruit here, and cheese and crackers." I recited the list of food, thinking of Josephine, whose refrigerator and kitchen shelves always overflowed with tasty leftovers and deli cold cuts and cheeses. Having enough to feed friends and family at a moment's notice was a lifetime commitment for my mother, but a landmark event for me.

An hour later, the four of us had reached reasonable agreement. I tried to assure Rose that I wouldn't take any risks. For all we knew, I reminded her, Congress-woman Hurley's death was a random hit-and-run and no one attending the wake would be the least bit dangerous.

Robert and Frank came up with some chores for me. My life was turning into a series of limited duties, I thought. I'd wear a small black ribbon with STAFF in silver letters, like the other Galigani employees, and help people find their way around the rooms. I'd watch for Father Tucci and take care of his hospitality. This would free up Martha to stay in the second-floor office and take phone calls. And—this was my major vic-tory—I would make sure the immediate family had water or tissues or whatever they needed.

I promised Rose I'd always stay within sight of Tony or Sal, the two largest men I'd ever seen, who were called in whenever crowd control might be needed.

Alone in my apartment, I rubbed my hands together in satisfaction and checked the time—5 P.M. I cleared the remains of our meal, simultaneously snacking on cannoli crumbs, and went to my closet to assemble an outfit befitting a staff member of a funeral home. *Black*, I thought, in a burst of brilliance, although Rose seldom wore black on these occasions. One-hundred-and-five-pound Rose, I reasoned, could pull off any look in any color, but I needed all the help I could get.

I chose a black three-piece ensemble, of the kind I favored—a skirt and long-sleeved blouse, with a coordinated vest trimmed in a silver print along the edges. I had long considered that vests were originally invented with me in mind, since I firmly believed that they hid all the unflattering bumps in my torso.

Before I finished dressing, the phone rang, and my earlier nightmare came true. Peter was calling, "to check on me."

"I thought I might come over this evening, if you happen to be free."

"I'm not, Peter," I said, trying to sound a bit disappointed. "I'm getting ready to attend a wake." I'd made a split-second decision to spare Peter the fact that I was actually preparing to work at a wake.

"That congresswoman?"

"Yes."

And once again, Peter's tone changed my mood in a matter of seconds. I no longer wanted to sound disappointed that I was busy, or even vaguely interested in a visit from him.

"I read that the police are considering foul play. Don't tell me you're involved in the investigation."

"I won't if you don't want me to, Peter."

"Why are you like that, Gloria? I'm just worried, after what happened last time."

"Last time worked out fine," I said, glad there was no video link to show Peter that I had automatically rubbed my wounded arm at the mention of "last time."

"Well, are you at least able to have lunch with me on Monday? I won't see you before Christmas otherwise. I'm going on the senior trip to Washington."

"How nice," I said. "I love Washington. The National Gallery, the Smithsonian."

"It's not the same with a hotel full of eighteen-year-olds that you're responsible for."

"I guess not." I removed the receiver from my ear and looked at it momentarily, as if to ask it why it was bothering me with these petty issues. I wasn't proud of my reaction to Peter, but the alternative of leading him to think I was still his girlfriend was out of the question. The fact that I'd been engaged to another man and then lived three thousand miles away since our last date didn't seem to faze him.

"So, lunch on Monday?"

"I'll let you know," I said. "I'm pretty busy with this case."

"Good night, Gloria. I can tell you're distracted right now."

"Good night, Peter." The growling sound I made came after I'd hung up.

I let out a big sigh and walked to my window to calm down. I could always count on a snowy street scene to soothe my nerves. Later, I decided, I'd have to think of a more permanent way to resolve my relationship with Peter.

I searched through my CDs for some technical-reading music. I still hadn't gone through Vincent Cavallo's report and hoped it would contain some physics that I could enjoy. Just picturing the helium atom, with its two lovely electrons, relaxed me.

To the tune of Beethoven's *Ninth Symphony*, I read another person's view of the helium operation. Since

Cavallo was a physicist, I wasn't surprised to find that he took the strong position of the American Physical Society. *"Profoundly concerned about the potential loss of the nation's accumulated helium reserves,"* were the words they used.

The body of the report listed several actions that Cavallo felt would improve the helium program. Among his recommendations were the elimination of smaller activities, like testing, that weren't cost effective, and charging higher fees to private industry for services. Cavallo estimated that the program would see an increase in income of four to eight million dollars, with a loss of only thirty jobs if his plan were followed.

I couldn't see anything suspicious in Cavallo's report. Even though his view was very biased in favor of upgrading instead of discontinuing the operation, it was hardly a motive for murder. Or maybe I was still suffering under the illusion that people dedicated to science were incapable of violence, especially murder.

The thought of murder brought me up short again, and I realized I hadn't taken any time to grieve over the death of a young woman. *Is this how homicide detectives get through their careers*, I wondered, *thinking of murder as a puzzle to be solved as opposed to a human death to be mourned?*

Whatever uncivil behavior she may have exhibited toward her family and friends, whatever her political leanings, Congresswoman Hurley didn't deserve to be murdered.

I cringed at the idea that my only concern about the

comings and goings of the Galigani hearse might be whether it would wake me in the middle of the night. A dead woman had been brought to a basement laboratory three floors below me, and it had taken me all this time to feel sorry for her and her family.

I packed up my notes and lay down on the couch as the ''Song of Joy'' came to an end.

Chapter Seven

My solemn mood persisted as I left my apartment and walked down Galigani's main stairway to the parlor where Congresswoman Margaret Hurley lay in her brown walnut casket. I remembered a line from a Jane Austen novel that had particular significance for me since I'd been dwelling in a funeral home—*"The living ever feel unease, when the dead are in residence."*

The fragrance of gladioli and mums, and the slow organ music piped through the rooms, didn't help my spirits. I loved cut flowers, but much to Frank's chagrin, I swore that they smelled different when arranged around a dead body.

I'd fallen asleep on my couch, and had to iron the telltale wrinkles from my skirt, thus missing my self-imposed starting time of six-thirty. *Great first impression if this were a real job*, I thought.

It was close to seven and several dozen people were

already in the parlor when I made my entrance. For the tenth time, I checked my little black Galigani ribbon, as if I'd just won first prize at a morbid science fair.

Rose's assistant, Martha, greeted me and pointed out Frances Whitestone.

"As long as you're here, I'll get back upstairs," Martha said in a normal tone. And then, in a whisper, "I know you're on this case. Good luck."

Martha had always overestimated my police involvement, once introducing me to her eight-year-old twin boys as "a policeperson." Usually I corrected her, but this time I simply thanked her, and gave her a smile and a wink that said "I'm on it."

Frances Whitestone would have been hard to pick out of a lineup as a senior citizen. Standing tall and straight, with her hair more red than gray, she wore her money well, from her simple sheath dress in dark green silk, to her rich-looking purse and shoes.

I had to adjust my old-woman image to accommodate this perfect picture of a wealthy widow of one of Boston's financial geniuses. My previous images came from my grandmother and older aunts—hair all gray, their short, wide bodies ensheathed in flowered housedresses and terry-cloth slippers.

A quick calculation told me that Frances Whitestone had to be close to eighty, given the number of years she and her late husband had dominated local politics from behind the scenes, funding winners almost every time. I sighed as I walked over to her, trying to formulate a word of sympathy that wouldn't sound hollow. I resolved to listen more closely to Frank in a situation like this, the next time I had the opportunity.

"Good evening, Mrs. Whitestone," I said, extending my hand. "I'm so sorry for your loss. I know how close you were to Margaret."

"Thank you," she said. She gave me an appraising look, up and down quickly, without moving her head, and then trained her eyes on my ribbon. "Are you aware that there are only two boxes of votive candles in this room?" she said. "Hardly enough. Can you see to it?"

"Right away," I said, feeling like I'd flunked a blood test, and guessing that I wouldn't be delivering any tissues to her chair.

Not that I was judging her grief. People mourn in different ways, I knew, and I had the feeling that all of Frances Whitestone's would be done in the privacy of her boudoir. My own relatives had preferred to express their suffering by throwing themselves, wailing, onto the casket of the departed loved one.

I desperately wanted to ask Mrs. Whitestone some questions, and had to clench my jaws and fists to keep from reading her my mental list. Had she heard the hit-and-run car drive away? Had she seen any suspicious-looking cars in the neighborhood that day? Who else knew what time Margaret would be arriving? How soon had she gone out to investigate the noise? I was aggravated that Matt hadn't even told me the basics yet, like who found the body.

The sight of Robert Galigani across the room reminded me that I was supposed to be working. I tried to figure out who was responsible for the votive lights and decided to take it to the top, or next to the top, to Robert himself. In the precomputer days, when people knew what carbon copies were, that's what we would have called Robert, so like his father in manner and looks. Unlike his journalist brother, Robert wore his hair in a neat, short cut, and except for minor glitches in vocabulary, like ''cool,'' had a professional manner at all times.

I noted with dismay that Robert was already starting to bald, and I had a moment of regret that I'd missed the childhood of Rose and Frank's children. I'd managed to keep a special connection with Mary Catherine, my godchild, but mostly through presents and phone calls. The longest time I'd ever spent with her was one summer when she stayed with me in California, during her antimother teen years.

These reflections were a small lapse in the otherwise great progress I'd been making since my return to Revere, controlling twinge-of-regret moments, replacing them with moments of excitement at new adventures, like dating and police work.

''Mrs. Whitestone would like to have more votive candles at the ready,'' I told Robert. ''If you tell me where they are, I'd be glad to get them.''

''Thanks, Gloria,'' he said. ''They're in the storage closet in the basement, next to the prep room.''

''Oh,'' I said, with a grimace that Robert seemed to recognize immediately. The whole family must know, I thought, that I was inordinately squeamish about going into the basement where the embalming process was carried out. I'd even started to take my dirty clothes to an outside Laundromat rather than use the washer and dryer in the room next to the prep room. It's a testimony to my fear that I preferred the spectacle of pulling up to a coin-operated facility and dragging my dirty laundry out of a new Cadillac.

"I'll send Tony," Robert said. "The boxes are heavy anyway."

So far, I thought, *I've arrived at work late and reneged on my first chore. It's a good thing I retired from my old job with a healthy pension.*

"Thanks," I said to Robert, and looked around for a less intimidating duty.

To my disappointment, there was not much action to this role of mortuary staff person. Although there were more guests than chairs, and the overflow spilled into the lobby, all of the visitors seemed self-sufficient and not very interesting, as far as what I'd come to call The Hurley Case.

I still hadn't laid eyes on Brendan Hurley, Margaret's brother. I thought it strange that he wasn't in charge of his sister's funeral services.

Although I kept checking the guest register, pretending to be tidying up the table, I'd seen no record of a visit by Vincent Cavallo from the Charger Street lab, or Patrick Gallagher, Margaret's ex-fiancé. Thanks to Rose, who sneaked looks at the tabloids in the supermarket, I was up-to-date on their headlines: *Dead Congresswoman Dumped Boyfriend for Job in D.C.*, and *Woman Rep Mocked Brother in Public*.

I didn't even have the pleasure of seeing Matt again that evening, since his partner showed up instead. Berger came over to me and I was at least grateful that we now seemed to be friends.

"I thought this would be a good chance to see the family," he said, "since I'm a little behind on this case. Haven't been getting much rest."

"Cynthia?" I asked.

Berger grinned his new-father grin again, and told me a few stories about Cynthia's cute sounds and movements.

I wanted to question Berger about the case—what was everyone's alibi, for example, and who were the leading suspects? Matt as much as admitted to me that they were thinking in terms of deliberate homicide and not random hit-and-run anymore. I decided not to disturb the delicate truce Berger and I had reached. I was relieved when he moved away to work the crowd, afraid that I might either inadvertently reveal how bored I was with his baby stories, or blurt out something intelligent like, "Do you think her spurned fiancé was angry enough to kill her?"

When Father Tucci, the pastor of St. Anthony's, finished the rosary, I made a fuss over him, because there wasn't much else to do. I served him coffee in the small downstairs office Frank and Robert used for seeing clients. The main offices on the second floor, where Rose and Martha carried out the bookkeeping and management operations, were off-limits during wake hours, as, of course, was the third floor, which housed only my apartment. I listened to the old priest's reports on the Christmas cake sale and the funding drive for the new rectory.

I was beginning to think that funeral-home employees spend most of their time standing around, listening to dull tales, when a general stirring of the population occurred. After the rosary, deliberately or not, Margaret Hurley's brother, Brendan, finally arrived, with a group of four men who made Tony and Sal look like kindergarten teachers.

"Hey, Buddy," I heard often as he walked into the parlor, shaking hands and bestowing small hand-waves on the crowd, his men around him like the Secret Service around the President. *You'd think he was the politician*, I thought, *rather than his sister*.

Buddy looked "dark Irish," as we on the Italian side of town used to call them. Unlike his fair-skinned sister, Buddy had almost-olive skin and dark brown hair. Only his green eyes and the enormous shamrock tie pin he wore gave away his ethnic background.

Buddy was made much of by everyone except Mrs. Whitestone. I remembered the casual remark Frank made about the bad feeling between Buddy and Frances Whitestone, and I felt I was seeing it firsthand. I wished I knew more, and plotted a way to find out. After all, he was on my list of duties, caring for immediate family. What care I could give Buddy, strutting boldly and powerfully toward his deceased sister, I couldn't imagine.

I zigzagged my way to Buddy and his group, now assembled around the casket, lighting candles and making sweeping signs of the cross in the vicinity of their enormous foreheads and chests.

When they'd turned back to the crowd, there I was, a head shorter than the shortest of them, ready to care for them.

"I'm Gloria Lamerino, Mr. Hurley," I said, my fingers brushing the Galigani ribbon, my heart beating a little more loudly than usual, I thought. "I'm sorry about your sister. If there's anything I can do . . ."

"Thanks," he said. I thought I heard "danks," but chalked it up to my imagination and my stereotyping of men in dark shirts and white ties, which was what Buddy and his crew were wearing.

Berger, on the job, I noticed, came over to the group, and introduced himself to Buddy. I wondered if Berger had read Buddy's statement, assuming he'd given one. I was getting more and more annoyed at how little I knew, and had to hold myself back from stomping to a phone to call Matt and demand some answers.

Next to Buddy was a man who looked at me a moment longer than he needed to, I thought. As we chatted about the tragic accident, and then about the weather, the man made nervous twitching motions, practically hopping from one foot to the other, like a seventh-grader who needed to use the boys' room. Buddy introduced him to me and Berger.

"This here's my friend Rocky Busso," he said, and the soundtrack of *The Godfather* played in my head.

Rocky seemed to have no neck, and I thought I

could see rippling muscles about to break through the sleeves of his dark jacket.

"Hello, Dr. Lamerino," he said.

"Rocky," I said, bravely offering my hand, and vaguely aware of a shiver that had started down my spine.

"I bet you're not used to this weather, huh? California's always seventy degrees, right?"

"Right," I said, as a second shiver made its way all through my body, so strong that I felt my skirt and vest must be showing visible signs of a wave as large as those at high tide on Revere Beach.

"Excuse me, please, I need to see if Father Tucci needs anything," I said, and walked away in what seemed like slow motion. I felt as I did often in dreams, when I'd keep running and running but stayed in the same spot.

I made my way to Tony, who was standing by the door to the foyer.

"I'm glad you're here, Tony," I said, touching his arm, feeling his muscle, as if to reassure myself that someone strong was on my side.

Chapter Eight

I climbed the two flights of stairs to my apartment, looking over my shoulder the whole way. Every time a step creaked under my foot, a tiny shiver went through me. It was only eight-thirty, but I completely abandoned the idea of staying at my post until the wake ended at nine.

I locked my door, then leaned against it, putting all my weight on its dark wood panels, as if that would help keep it locked. I breathed deeply and remembered that after my break-in two months ago, Matt had a police security expert install the latest in locks—a deadbolt with hardened steel inserts, and a specially designed strike plate anchored into the building frame. I felt better thinking of that, but only marginally. For all I knew, Rocky had a key.

I walked to my window and looked down on Tuttle Street. Thanks to the celebrity of the deceased, Frank had arranged for around-the-clock police presence, and the sight of a white-and-red Revere Police car and two uniformed officers brought my breathing to a normal level. I inhaled as hard as I could, as if to suction their strength and protection up through the wintry air and into my living room. At a certain angle, I could see my reflection in the window. My hair looked grayer and my jowls more droopy, and I seemed to have aged a decade since meeting Rocky. My "staff" ribbon was slightly askew, as if it, too, had suffered a blow.

Following a curious habit of mine whenever I entered a hotel room for the first time, I walked through my apartment, checking under my bed and in my closets, and even under the sink. I'd carried out this procedure once when sharing a suite with Elaine at a conference in San Jose.

"I thought physicists were supposed to be logical," Elaine had said. "What are you going to do if you find someone?"

I had no sensible defense, but that never kept me from completing my search, then or now. Maybe it was just to eliminate the element of surprise, I'd decided. *If you're here, I want to know now.*

In another display of faulty logic, I put on a CD of light Christmas music, to ward off pending evil. Surely, I reasoned, no harm could come to someone in her own living room listening to "I Saw Mommy Kissing Santa Claus." I resolved to put up a Christmas tree, too, for further protection, although I'd been resisting the effort that would take.

The hardest chore was entering the narrow hallway

that ran the length of my bedroom and living room—a curious structural feature of my apartment. A trap door in the ceiling of the two-foot wide corridor provided access to the attic, which had been the scene of the only physical violence I've ever experienced. It was enough for a lifetime, however, and I hadn't been in the attic since a bullet bounced off my shoulder and into its wall.

I took a flashlight and made my way up the short ladder that was designed to hook into slots on the attic floor. I trained my light around the musty loft, coughed out some dust, and saw that it was empty except for Galigani memorabilia and the boxes I'd kept there in storage. My eyes fell on the cartons labeled AG in thick black marker, and I remembered finding Al's book, retrieved from the pocket of his robe in one of the boxes.

Back in my living room, I checked again on the officers below my window and decided I'd had enough of fearful cowering for one night. I tried to convince myself that I was overreacting. For one thing, I told myself, it was entirely possible that Rocky had overheard someone say I'd just come from California, or that I was a "Doctor." But I didn't really think so. To my knowledge, I'd never laid eyes on either Buddy or Rocky until that moment, and they had only been in the parlor a matter of minutes.

I needed to get to the bottom of Rocky Busso. In the safety of my flat, with no one under my sink, and two policemen within shouting distance, I was beginning to be angry at him. If he was deliberately trying to intimidate me, it had worked for a while.

I always considered myself a neat person, and this situation was remarkably untidy. Could the threads of my investigations, as slight as they were so far, be intertwined? I wondered. The idea that there was a connection between Hurley's death two days ago and Al's thirty-four years ago seemed even more far-fetched than a female pope before I died.

First, how did he know me? The only possible connection was Al Gravese. Maybe Rocky's organization, as I chose to call it, had a tap on the *Journal*'s micro-fiche system, and when I accessed the records for 1962, an alarm went off in a dark, smoky room over a bar. Too far-out, I thought, but I had to start somewhere.

Al's book was in my briefcase, with the *Journal* articles I'd printed out. I piled the notebook and papers on my kitchen table, which was actually at the edge of my living room, prepared a snack of cannoli and coffee, and set to work.

I got out my best magnifying glass, with a battery-operated light attached, and studied the photos in the articles. The crash had occurred in the Point of Pines section of Revere, at the northern end of the city, where it meets Saugus. It was a single-car accident, in which Al's enormous Buick sedan apparently flew off the road and fell into the Pines River. The photos were mostly of the crash scene, with only one of Al, taken when he won a prize for his tulips at Boston's Horti-cultural Show.

I sat back in my chair, swallowing the last daub of cream cheese from the cannoli, and asked myself how I expected to recognize Rocky Busso as he looked thirty-four years ago. Al was ten years older than me, thirty-one at the time of his death. If Rocky were the same age, he'd be sixty-six now. I didn't think so. But, from what I remembered of his slightly graying hair and leathery face, he could be in his early fifties, making him Al's teenaged friend.

After a half-hour of racking my brain for ideas, I came up with: check the 1962 *Boston Globe* for photos, since Al was living in Boston's North End, not Revere, when he died; ask Frank, who'd lived in Revere all his life, if he'd ever seen Rocky or any of Buddy's other escorts before this evening; and check the *Journal*'s crime pages for any mention of Rocky Busso.

It took a brief stretching session to ease my stiffness, and another glance at the police car for me to get to the obvious. I opened Al's book and looked under B. And there it was: *Rocky Busso, 555-6754, $100.*

Before I could talk myself out of it, I picked up my phone and pushed the numbers. I heard only one ring, then a machine hookup. I recognized the voice as that of a generic answering service, and hung up with relief. I certainly didn't know what I would have said if a real person had answered.

Less than a minute later, at 9:44 by the digital clock on my desk, my phone rang, and I flinched as if I'd been stung by an insect. I carried the phone to the window before pushing the talk button. As I watched the tiny red light on the front panel run back and forth, seeking the best channel, I felt my heartbeat following the same pattern.

"Hello," I said, when the light stopped and my pulse settled on a steady rate. I heard the catch in my throat, and cleared it as softly as I could.

"Hello, I hope I'm not waking you."

When I heard Matt's voice, I dropped into my rocker with such force, it almost glided off its tracks.

"I figured you'd be down at the wake until nine or so," he said.

"As a matter of fact, I came up a little early," I said. "I can barely hear you, by the way. Are you in your car?"

"Yes, I'm down by Starbucks. If it's not too late, I'd like to bring you a cappuccino."

"By all means," I said, thinking *"Yippee!"*

"See you in fifteen minutes."

I nearly skipped around my apartment, straightening the pillows on my couch, clearing away the evidence of my snack, and running a brush through my unruly wavy hair, which was a week past its optimum short length. I considered adding a squirt of cologne, but decided that would be too obvious, especially since I very seldom used it. I settled on shaking the crumbs from the creases of my skirt and smoothing out my vest, since I didn't have time to change.

On my way to the CD player to switch to a jazz disc that Matt had given me, I heard the buzz from the intercom that connects all the offices and my apartment, a remnant of the days when a caretaker lived on my floor.

I pushed RECEIVE on the unit at the back of my desk and heard Rose's voice. Within just a few minutes, my apartment and my mood had brightened considerably, as if someone had thrown a switch and introduced extra lighting.

"Gloria, are you all right?" she asked. "Robert said you went upstairs early and looked sick or upset."

"I'm fine," I said. "I'll explain tomorrow. I'm sorry I fell down on the job. You must be exhausted."

"There are still a few people around outside, but we've just closed the parlors."

"Is Buddy still there?" I asked, amazed at my own question.

"No, he came late and left early. Why do you ask?"

"No reason," I lied, justifiably, I thought, since I didn't want to worry her.

"Well, we were going to come up," Rose said, "but I think we'll just head home. Did you see the police car? They're going to be there all night, just so you know."

"Frank told me," I said. "And there's going to be another one out there shortly, an unmarked one."

"Matt's coming?" Rose was quick, and the delight in her voice, echoing from the tinny intercom speaker, embarrassed me. "Now we're definitely not coming up," she said.

"It's probably business," I said, suppressing a grin, as if she could see my expression.

"I'll expect a report in the morning."

"You'll have one."

Matt appeared on my doorstep carrying a cardboard tray with two paper cups bearing a familiar logo. He was still in work clothes, dark suit and tie and the raincoat that looked like he'd purposely wrinkled it to match Columbo's.

"I got in just before they closed," he said.

"This is wonderful," I said, taking the tray, leaving him to wonder whether I meant him or the espresso drinks.

"I decided it was time to brief you on a few things," Matt said. "Since this has officially become a murder investigation."

My pleasure at finally being brought in on the case overcame any disappointment I felt that Matt hadn't just dropped in for a casual social visit.

We sat in the rockers with our coffees, a plate of cheese and crackers and fruit on the low table in front of us. I liked the idea that for once I had something to serve an unannounced guest, and resolved to stop and shop more often.

I wasn't sure whether I was going to say anything about Rocky. Certainly Matt's presence in my living room had made the event seem far away and insignificant.

In any case, there seemed to be more tangible connections to pursue in the Hurley case.

"I called Carey in Texas," Matt said, "since he was on Hurley's calendar for next week. I assumed she was going to travel there, but I learned that their meeting was here. Carey's at the new Beach Inn.''

''Here in town?''

''Here in town.''

''He was in Revere on Sunday evening?''

''He was.''

I settled back in my rocker and took a sip of foam. Matt had shaken a generous amount of chocolate on it, just as I liked it. He was looking at me as if we were playing Twenty Questions and it was my turn.

''Did you talk to him?''

''I did.''

''Did he have a rental car?'' I asked, and his body language told me that was the right question.

''Yes.''

''Something big and heavy, not a compact?''

''Yes.''

''Did you track it down?'' Now we were both smiling at the course of the conversation.

''Yes.''

''And what shape is it in?''

''It had a busted front bumper. Carey said he's not used to driving in snow and he ran into a tree.''

Chapter Nine

For a while, I felt like Matt's partner. He asked me to accompany him when he went to talk to Carey at his Chelsea plant on Wednesday afternoon. He'd be asking questions about CompTech's helium contracts, and thought it would be useful to have me there as a technical consultant. So did I.

"Can't your lab people tell if Carey's car hit a tree or another car?" I asked.

"We're looking at it, but Carey brought the car in right away, so that trail is dead. The Revere Rents mechanic wasn't paying attention to details like that. He just straightened the car out and painted over the problems. We're lucky anyone remembered that Carey turned in a damage report."

"That was fast. I wish my mechanics were that swift and thorough."

Matt laughed and took out his notebook, apparently

still up for business conversation. He flipped through the pages, densely packed with writing and doodles.

"I assume you're ready to ask Carey some specifics about the contracts?"

"Absolutely," I said, calculating how many hours were left to do a bit of cramming. The meeting wasn't until one o'clock. Plenty of time, I thought.

In the spirit of our partnership, I asked Matt about the alibis of the likely suspects. Not that physics gives you any better training in logic than detective work, but I knew Matt liked to bounce his reasoning off me. In the last two months, I'd often thought that my timing couldn't have been better—I showed up just as he was losing his partner, at least temporarily.

I got a notepad of my own, ready for Matt's briefing.

"Carey says he was in his room at the Beach Inn all evening. Ate a room-service dinner. So far, that checks out, but we can't be sure he didn't leave for a while to drive over to Oxford Park."

The inn was near the overpass on the Revere/Chelsea line, so, with icy roads, I figured Carey would have needed close to forty-five minutes for the round trip. I made some columns on my notepad, and started filling in data, feeling the rush I always got from collecting and organizing information.

"Patrick Gallagher, the ex-boyfriend," Matt continued. "Said he was at the Northgate mall shopping by himself until it closed at nine, then home to watch television. Turns out that although it was Sunday, the mall was open that late—extended hours in December.

We're looking into some witnesses who can place him there. Says he didn't buy anything, was just looking.

"Buddy was playing cards in a clubroom with a group of buddies, pardon the pun. And they were surrounded by about a dozen people playing pool and drinking. His alibi is the most solid at the moment.

"And that about covers the money, passion, domestic discord trio of motives. Mrs. Whitestone, who's not exactly a prime suspect anyway, was at home waiting for Margaret. She's making a fuss because we still have Margaret's personal effects, including the luggage and the bags of Christmas presents. She thinks we should release everything that's personal, but of course we can't do that yet."

"She's not even a relative," I said. "But she looks like a woman who's used to getting her own way."

"Seems so," Matt said, sticking his notebook into his back pocket. "The Whitestones have dominated politics around here for a long time."

I cleared my throat, ready to change the subject.

"What about Buddy's friends?" I asked. "He came in tonight with an entourage of strongmen."

"You mean maybe he hired someone? Always a possibility. With luck that would turn up in his bank records."

"Unless he paid him cash."

"You sound like you have someone in mind," Matt said.

"One of the men there tonight impressed me as capable of making such a deal," I said, wondering if my voice sounded as shaky to Matt as it did to me.

Matt took out his notebook again.

"You have good instincts," he said. "Do you have a name for this man?"

"Rocky Busso." I neglected to say that I had his telephone number, too, and perhaps his weekly salary as a teenager in 1962.

"I'll check with Berger, too," Matt said. "Maybe he noticed something. Did you see Berger there tonight?"

"I did."

"I'm glad you two are getting along," Matt said, getting up and stretching his arms out to the side. His jacket fell open, putting his hefty middle at my eye level. It was still tight enough not to creep over his belt, I noted, sucking in my own middle. Matt wandered around the room, rubbing his temples and rolling his head around his neck. I had the feeling I'd been invited to his warm-up routine. I almost invited him to use my exercise bicycle, which was still as good as new.

I found myself following him around with my eyes, trying to see my apartment as he saw it. I hoped he liked my set of California posters, framed in a light wood, a present from my West Coast friends when I left my Berkeley lab. I also hoped he wouldn't lean on a dusty surface. I was sure he cared that I hadn't done any housework in days. Fortunately, at five-six, he was too short to lean on the top shelf of my bookcase.

"I know George can be tough," he said, coming perilously close to the tiny gray dustballs behind my

computer monitor, "but I hated seeing antagonism between my partner and my . . ."

I could hardly wait for the next word, hoping for
the middle-aged equivalent of "girlfriend," willing to
settle for anything more personal than "consultant."
What I heard was neither.

"What's all this?" he asked.

Matt had exercised his way over to my kitchen table, where my Al Gravese research project was spread
out. He fingered the articles and looked at me, his tone
changing to one of minor disapproval.

"A little investigation of your own, I see," he said.

I went over to the table and picked up the articles,
tapping them on the table to line up the sheets of paper, as if they represented a completed term paper I
was about to hand in to the teacher. *Is this the moment
I've been waiting for,* I asked myself—*do I ask Matt
for the help I need from him, or do I cover this up
and pretend I'm into nostalgia?* One thing I didn't
want was to anger Matt. He'd been angry with me
before when I overstepped my "limited basis" contract, and it was not a happy memory.

I remembered an early conversation with Matt and
hoped he did, too.

"I think I told you," I said. "I've always wondered
whether Al's crash was really an accident."

"Yes, you did tell me. And I know there was an
inquiry. Were you interviewed at the time?"

"I was. Two detectives came to my home. I was
living with my father, on Tuckerman Street. They
asked if I'd ever met any of Al's friends, if I knew

how he'd spent the day that Friday, what I knew of his financial situation, that kind of thing. It's funny how little I remember of it. I guess I was too shocked to realize what was happening. Not to mention dumb and naive.''

''Don't forget young,'' Matt said. ''How old were you, about twenty?''

''Is that a guess or a calculation?'' I asked, in a attempt to lighten the moment.

''I wasn't trying to pry.''

''I don't mind if you do. Yes, I was twenty.''

''At the time, most of us on the force thought there was some connection there.''

''It's kind of you not to specify the connection. It was only much later when I thought about the detectives' questions that I saw where they were going with the interview. For the most part, I'm reading these for the first time,'' I said, pointing to the neat pile of microfiche copies. ''How did I miss what everyone else seemed to know about Al?''

I hadn't intended to bring Matt in on my quest in such a personal way. I wanted his help with the investigation, not with sorting out my feelings and regrets. At least that's what I thought.

''Don't be hard on yourself, Gloria. It was a different era. Especially for women.''

''It certainly was,'' I said, surprised and pleased that he noticed.

It was Matt's turn to clear his throat.

''Now, Gloria,'' he started, with a fatherly edge to his voice, ''I can see why you'd be curious about your fiancé's death, but suppose he was connected? It could be dangerous for you to go digging around."

I wanted to correct him with "late fiancé," but I thought it would put too much emphasis on my current availability. I wasn't that much of a feminist, I'd learned, when it came to dating protocol.

"I was hoping to confine my digging to police records," I said. "Nothing hazardous to my health."

Matt gave a hearty laugh.

"If I didn't know better, I'd think you were hanging around me just to take advantage of my badge."

All of my internal organs twitched at "hanging around," and I desperately wanted his definition of the phrase, but I stopped myself. *This is not a physics class,* I told myself. *We're not talking about Newton's laws.*

"I hope you do know better," I said.

Matt's look and smile told me all was well, and I imagined this to be the point in a romantic comedy where we rushed into each other's arms.

Not tonight, however, because Matt had made his way to my phone. Al's little notebook was next to it, open to B.

After a mental gasp, I had what I thought of as a stroke of sheer brilliance.

"I've been meaning to show you this," I said, scooping up the book, closing it at the same time. "It was Al's. I found it when I was going through his things in the attic."

"Al's book? Something the police never saw?"

"That's right," I said. "I left some boxes with Rose

and Frank when I went to California, and I'm just getting around to sorting through them.''

Matt had resumed his exercise mode, pacing and scratching his head.

"And you had some of Al's things?" he asked.

"I didn't know I did, at least I didn't remember."

So far, I couldn't hear any reproach in his voice, and I continued with my very reasonable explanation.

"Our old landlord lived upstairs from me and my father, and he used to let Al stay with him if we came home late, so he wouldn't have to drive all the way to the North End. Al kept a few things up there and Mr. Corrado gave them to me in a sealed bag, after Al died.''

"And the police wouldn't have thought to search your house."

"No, I guess not."

"And it never occurred to you to tell them about the bag?''

"I told you, I wasn't thinking straight at the time."

I didn't like Matt's tone or mine, but I didn't seem to have any control over either one.

"I'm going to take this," Matt said, putting Al's book in his already bulging jacket pocket. "I'm sure you have no use for it?''

I swallowed hard, hearing an exclamation point at the end of his last remark, though it was disguised as a question.

"So, what does this mean about the police files?" I asked. I had nothing to lose, I thought, since the romantic atmosphere had already been shattered.

"I'll think about it," he said, and moved toward the door.

"I'll see you at one tomorrow," I said, hopeful that he wouldn't cancel his invitation to go with him to Carey's plant.

"Right," he said, "Good night, Gloria."

I closed and locked the door behind him. *This guy is the master of abrupt departures,* I thought. *And I'm only slightly better off now than before he came. I have a little more information about the Hurley case, but I don't have Al's book and I don't have a good feeling about our relationship.*

At least one thing had worked in my favor—after a lifetime of working in science and mathematics, I had excellent recall for numbers.

I took a pad of paper and pencil and wrote down *R. B., 555-6754.*

Chapter Ten

Thanks to a few unsettling dreams, I woke up several times during the night. In one dream, I was at Al's wake and hundreds of people were pointing at me, accusing me of killing him. In another, Rocky Busso was pushing Josephine over a cliff on the Pacific Ocean, at the edge of San Francisco, where the real-life Josephine had never stepped foot. Just before I woke, I dreamed I was talking into my telephone, but no sound came out.

Why don't I ever have pleasant dreams, I wondered, *like an image of Matt folding his napkin, saying, "that was the best snack I ever had," and "I love you, Gloria"?* I considered calling Elaine in Berkeley and asking her opinion, since she had a strong belief in the connection between our dreams and our inner lives.

That notion didn't get very far, and instead I sat at my desk to do a morning's work. I had Carey's contracts to go through, and it was about time I'd given a little attention to my presentation for Peter's students, only a few days away.

So far, all I'd done was choose the quote I would use to open the class, Marconi's own observation on his invention of the radio: "My chief trouble was that the idea was so elementary, so simple in logic, that it seemed difficult to believe no one else had thought of putting it into practice." Not a bad thing for a homicide investigator to keep in mind, either, I thought.

I started with the pile of consulting agreements from Hurley's briefcase. I made a list of questions I had for Carey, including the nature of the computer upgrades and the training classes he'd contracted for. I had a hard time weeding out the substance from the legal boilerplate.

About an hour later, I felt I was ready for the Chelsea meeting and called down on the intercom to see if Rose had time for a coffee break.

"You bet," she said. "I can't wait to hear about last night."

"You're not going to be happy," I said.

"I'm coming up anyway."

While I waited for Rose, I started the coffee, loaded my papers into my briefcase, and brought out my file on Peter's class. I prepared a plate of food, assembling the one cannoli I had left, along with some fruit. The presentation left a lot to be desired, and I whined to myself about how little talent I had for such tasks. I could picture the same tidbits in Rose's hands, looking like the cover of an expensive coffee-table book.

* * *

A rare sight greeted me when I opened the door—
Rose in jeans and a California sweatshirt that I'd sent
her, with a green-and-white bandanna wrapped artfully
around her hair. Rose seldom wore anything but professional attire around the mortuary, but even in her
work clothes she looked ready for visitors. I was sorry
that I was in jeans and a sweatshirt, too, since I hated
the comparisons I always made when Rose and I wore
similar outfits.

"We haven't had so many guests since we waked
Bishop Donovan," she said. "I decided to help a little
with the cleanup. The foyer was a mess from people
tracking in slush."

"You don't look like you've been mopping up
slush."

"I haven't. I've been doing everything else while
Martha and Tony take care of the slush—I cleaned
around the flowers, scraped the wax from the candle
rack, did a little vacuuming. Gloria, don't you think
I've earned a break?"

"More than I have. The only exercise I've had is
getting from my bed to my desk."

"So tell me," Rose said, cutting off a well-deserved
slice of cannoli.

I knew exactly what she meant, so I got to the point.

"We talked business," I said, "about the Hurley
case."

"That's it?"

"That's it. Except, he took Al's book."

Rose sat back, a look of smug relief creeping over her face.

"I'm glad. It's a job for professionals, Gloria. Here's my dream. You met Matt through some police work, but now you forget about that and settle down with him. Maybe buy that little house for sale across from us on Proctor. Do a little teaching on the side."

Rose brushed some crumbs from her jeans, and folded her arms as if she'd just made an incontestable judicial decision. She seemed pleased with the details of my life as she'd just planned it. Her courtlike demeanor didn't last very long, however.

"I did have one little thing to share with you," she said, leaning her body toward mine where we sat on the couch. We both twisted our necks around in a playful gesture, as if scanning the room for eavesdroppers.

"After you left, Hurley's ex-fiancé came by."

"Patrick Gallagher?"

"The same. He strolled right up to the casket, knelt down, and started sobbing and talking loudly—to the deceased."

I'd noticed that none of the Galiganis ever used words like corpse, or body, preferring more abstract phrases like "the deceased" or "departed loved one." It was easier to learn the language of quantum mechanics, I thought, than that of policemen and funeral directors.

I wanted to know more about Gallagher, and figured it was useless to try to hide my interest from Rose.

"Go on, Rose," I said, rotating my hand like a camerawoman on a live shoot.

"Well, it was obvious that he'd been drinking," Rose said. "Luckily, Tony was right there to handle him, but Frances Whitestone was livid."

"Is that all? Did you hear anything he said?"

"I've been saving that," Rose said. "He kept saying, 'I'm sorry, sweetheart, I'm so sorry.' "

Rose sat back with a satisfied look on her face. My heart went out to her as I realized the conflict she had between wanting me out of the homicide business, and needing to share with me whatever she knew, just in case it would help me.

"Thanks, Rose," I said.

After Rose left, I worked on Peter's class, just enough to ward off the panicky feeling I was getting with only four days till my appearance on Monday. Cruising the waves of the Internet, I located a source of old diagrams showing Marconi's early wireless systems, and typed out a few pages of notes on his work as a delegate to the peace conference at the end of World War I. I hadn't resolved the question I had about whether to mention his support of Mussolini.

I had to keep reminding myself how young Peter's students were, juniors and seniors in high school. I was sure they thought that the wars my peers and I lived through were in the same timeframe as the Trojan War.

While I had the files out, I decided to organize the rest of the series. I'd told Peter I'd give him a list, outlining six classes to take us through the rest of the school year. After Marconi, I planned to introduce the inventor of the battery, Alessandro Volta, in February, followed by Avogadro, Da Vinci, Galvani, and Torricelli. I'd close with one of my personal favorites, Maria Agnesi, an extraordinarily accomplished eighteenth-century mathematician.

At noon, when the phone rang, I was still in my jeans. I wasn't over being a little touchy about answering my phone, afraid that Rocky Busso might have used a code to determine who called him last night without leaving a message. Technology, which I usually embraced wholeheartedly, was beginning to show me its dark side.

No problem this time, however, as I heard Matt's voice.

"Is there a change of plan?" I asked.

"No, we're still on for one o'clock, in my office. But I wanted to ask you about this weekend. Some civic group came by here this morning offering us tickets to the *Messiah* concert by the Handel-Haydn Society. I guess it's be-kind-to-policemen week. Anyway, I thought I heard you and Rose say you'd like to go sometime, so I picked up four tickets for Saturday evening. What do you think?"

"I think they'll be thrilled," I said, welcoming a pleasant twinge. "I certainly am."

"Good. Do you have time to check with them? Maybe we can have dinner in Boston near the concert hall?"

It never occurred to me that a native of the Back

Bay wouldn't be familiar with the name and location of Boston's Symphony Hall, but it was a great testimony to Matt's willingness to learn new things. We'd been to two jazz concerts, which he loved, and I guessed he thought it was my turn.

"I'll take care of that part," I said.

"Good," Matt said again, showing the limitations of his social vocabulary. "I'll see you at one."

It seemed only right to bring Rose in on this. As I called down to her, I had a flashback to high school when we'd walk home together as far as we could go, then call each other as soon as we got in the door. At that time, it would be something really important, like "what are you going to wear to the party?"

This time seemed equally important, and I wasn't surprised at the lilt in Rose's voice when I laid out the plans.

"Gloria, how exciting."

"Yes, considering that the first time we talked about doing this, Peter was the fourth person in the group."

"Do you think Peter will remember?"

"Probably. I can hardly wait till he does."

"Well, I can hardly wait till Saturday," Rose said. "What are you going to wear to the party?"

I had to cut short Rose's elaborate wardrobe plans. No, I'd told her, there was not time before Saturday evening to shop for a new outfit.

I went to my bedroom to dress for my Chelsea meeting, humming the Hallelujah chorus on the way. I wasn't sure why Matt didn't wait an hour to tell me about the *Messiah* tickets. I ran through a list of possible reasons. Maybe he didn't want to mix business with pleasure; maybe he thought my calendar might fill up during the noon hour; maybe he was as excited as I was about our date. The last one was a risky thought, but I took it as a good sign that it even came to my mind.

My cold-weather clothes selections were dismal, and I reconsidered a shopping trip with Rose. I had a charcoal gray wool suit that fit me only within a fraction of an inch before my last cannoli, but I gave it a try. With an overblouse, it would do. I chose a silver mohair knit top, added a strand of hematite beads, and looked for a lapel pin. I knew I had one that would be appropriate for a meeting at CompTech—a small computer chip encased in a pewter frame.

I searched through my pins without success. Just as I was about to give up on finding the chip pin, I remembered that my jewelry box had an extra layer, a narrow one, almost like a false bottom. I picked up the top section, and there on the bottom was the tiny piece of computer jewelry, among earring parts and other notions.

As I reassembled my jewelry box, I had a fleeting image of something with similar construction. I stopped for a minute to clear my head and remembered why this activity seemed so familiar. During the brief period that I'd worked on classified material at the Berkeley lab, I was given a special briefcase, one with a false bottom as an extra safeguard. The idea was that, if a spy held me at gunpoint and searched my briefcase, he would find only meaningless unclassified reports. The secret restricted data, SRD we called it, was hidden underneath.

I drove to Matt's office much too quickly, considering the road conditions, picturing Margaret Hurley's wide briefcase and imagining what could be under the first layer.

I could tell that at first Matt thought the idea was on the wild side, but he humored me.

"How would we get at it?" he asked, looking at the lining of the apparently empty case, open on his lap.

We fiddled with the edges for a while; and then, from sheer luck, hit the right combination of pressure points, and the bottom came loose at the corners. We lifted the top section from the case.

On the next level, against a maroon felt backdrop, was a manila file folder labeled *Personal Correspondence*.

Matt gave me a wonderful smile, and then uttered one of my favorite expressions.

"Nice work, Gloria," he said.

Chapter Eleven

I stood with my hands behind my back, like a child waiting for a treat, while Matt thumbed through the papers in the file. Finally he spread them out on his desk and invited me to look at them with him.

The folder contained five letters to Hurley, with responses clipped to two of them. Two letters were from Patrick Gallagher, two from Vincent Cavallo, and one from Bill Carey. None from Buddy or Rocky. *Maybe they can't write*, I thought.

We read the letters quickly, swapping pages and mumbling out loud as we went along.

Two short letters from Patrick Gallagher carried the threat of suicide if Hurley didn't take him back. *"How can you let a career in corruption keep us apart,"* were his exact words in one of them.

Two long letters, several pages each, from Vincent Cavallo, were reasoned pleas for Hurley to reconsider his proposal for upgrading the helium facility instead of scrapping it. Hurley had attached her responses with paper clips. Put briefly, the answer was no.

The letter from Carey was the most revealing. It read, in part: *"I strongly urge you to continue the relationship you've had with our firm. I'm sure neither of us would profit from letting your colleagues or the general public in on our agreements."*

"So, Hurley got him the contracts in the first place," I said.

"Something to ask him about," Matt said, checking his watch. "How convenient that we're on our way to Chelsea."

We rode in one of the RPD's unmarked sedans, a beige four-door decorated with white swirls from the remains of snow and rock salt. It occurred to me that Matt and I did a lot of our talking in cars. I was beginning to know his right profile very well, from the tiny mole on his ample Roman nose to the wrinkled collar of his soft blue shirt. More often than not, we were on the way to or from interviews with murder suspects. It worried me a little that I liked this getting-to-know-you scenario more than the usual ones, like cocktail talk or blind dates.

"Did you have a chance to ask Rose or Frank about Saturday night?" Matt asked.

"Yes, they're free and would love to go," I said, understating Rose's excitement by a lot. "I'm looking forward to hearing the new and improved audio system that Symphony Hall has been advertising."

"I don't do this very often, you know."

"You mean fraternize with your PSAs?" I asked, referring to our Personal Services Agreement.

"That, too," he said, with a laugh.

"I hope you like it. You can have a preview if you like—I have *The Messiah* on disc."

"Maybe I'll do that. Are you as good at teaching music as you are science?"

Blushing is not as bad when you're in a car, I thought, *and maybe that's why I like this side-by-side arrangement.*

"Thanks," I said. "I hope I've been some help."

Matt turned to look at me briefly.

"More than you know," he said, and this time I was sure he caught my blush.

When we pulled into the parking lot at CompTech, I was almost relieved. I didn't know how many compliments I could take from Matt in one day.

CompTech was behind a market I remembered going to as a child with Josephine. I had a clear memory of standing in line with her to exchange stamps for government-controlled items like butter and sugar. Like my other memories of World War II, however, I wasn't sure whether I actually experienced the event or simply thought I did because I'd heard the stories over and over. Well into my teens in the late fifties, my aunts and uncles spoke of victory gardens, stamps for gasoline and alcohol, and ticker-tape parades as if they'd happened the day before.

CompTech's Chelsea operation was unimposing— a small office off a reception area, and a modest manufacturing section at the back. All the doors were open, and every room was visible from where we stood in the foyer.

The noisy back room had a dark concrete floor, lined with bulky metal tables. Men and women in unisex gray overalls sat on stools and in front of workbenches cluttered with tools and papers. A far cry from what I'd pictured when I thought of computer manufacturing—I'd envisioned rows of silent workers, clad in white from head to toe, in a meticulously clean room, using nanosized instruments.

"We have an appointment with Mr. Carey," Matt told the young receptionist, as if we couldn't see him, all six-one of him, standing behind the desk in an office a few feet away.

Carey was on the telephone, motioning to us with his free hand to enter. The receptionist seemed insistent on protocol, however, and ushered us in with a slight bow.

Near the door was an open box full of circuit boards in the shade of green familiar to anyone who's looked at the innards of a computer or any other piece of nineties electronics.

"This is all we do here," Carey said, pointing to the box and anticipating my question. He'd come around the front of the desk, towering over both of us.

"Just the boards. The chips are made at our main plant in Amarillo. We have three hundred thousand square feet down there in Texas," he said, feeding into my stereotype that everything in the Lone Star State is enormous. Carey certainly was—as wide as a steer,

I thought, with a healthy amount of dark brown hair and a flat, square face with enough wrinkles to put him at about sixty years old, I guessed.

I looked around for a ten-gallon hat on a coat rack somewhere, but didn't find one. I did see the traditional bolo tie around Carey's neck, however, a thick black cord with a large turquoise-and-silver ornament that looked out of place in Chelsea.

"You're Sgt. Gennaro, I presume," he said, taking Matt's hand. I hoped he didn't crush my boss and friend. "And you're Miss—?" This last query was directed at me, but before I could recover from his enthusiastic Southern drawl, Matt introduced me.

"This is my technical consultant, Dr. Gloria Lamerino," he said.

I thought I saw Carey's eyebrows go up a notch, but it may have been my biased imagination.

We took seats around the desk in the small office. What motif there was leaned decidedly toward southwestern, with geometric patterns the colors of sand and pastels in the carpet, and Native American art on the walls.

"I'm afraid we're not set up for the kind of hospitality we could show you down in the Panhandle," Carey said, "but I can have Miss Lacey get you a cup of coffee."

We shook our heads "no thank you," and exchanged a few more pleasantries about the Massachusetts weather. Then Matt assumed his business posture, his right leg crossed over his left, his notebook on the newly made lap.

"What was your relationship to Congresswoman Hurley?" Matt asked.

"Why, I didn't really have one to speak of," Carey said. "Of course, we met during the course of business now and then."

"The business being the federal government's helium operation?"

"That's right."

"Tell us about your contracts with the program," Matt said, sounding as casual as if he were interviewing a celebrity for a general interest magazine.

"Oh, we have a contract or two with them, has to do with computers and such. Lots of folks do. Universities, laboratories."

"I noticed that you're installing upgrades in the software and adding memory boards," I said. "Sixty-four megs of RAM on each of three dozen PCs since last fall. Isn't that overkill for a simple database system?"

"Especially one that might close this year?" Matt added. I'd resolved to leave the political phrases to him.

"That surely has not been decided," Carey said, stiffening, and converting his relaxed smile into a tight-lipped frown. "That project is one of the few examples of government gone right. They provide a valuable service to private buyers, for one thing."

"Not since the new source was discovered in Wyoming more than twenty years ago," I said, noticing both Carey's and Matt's eyebrows go up this time. It bothered me to be arguing against the helium operation, but I felt it was necessary to smoke out Carey's vested interest, and therefore his motive for murder. "That source amounts to about two hundred billion cubic feet of helium, and the total worldwide consumption is less than four billion cubic feet a year."

While I was rattling off numbers that I'd boned up on that morning, Matt was waiting to zero in on his real question. He took out the letter we'd found in the hidden compartment of Hurley's briefcase and handed it to Carey.

"Can you explain this letter, Mr. Carey?"

Carey handed the letter back to Matt, holding it by one edge as if it might be contaminated, or, I thought, evidence in a murder trial.

"I have no comment," he said.

"It looks to me like you and the congresswoman had something going that you didn't want to end," Matt said. "You contracted for more than two million dollars last year alone. Maybe Ms. Hurley was starting to worry about her conflict of interest?"

"And maybe I misunderstood the nature of this call," he said.

Carey stood up, looming over the neat desk. He buttoned his jacket in a gesture of closure.

"This conversation is over until my attorney is present," he said. "Leave your card with Miss Lacey and she'll call you to schedule an appointment."

I admired Matt's response under the circumstances, showing that he was more accustomed to this kind of abrupt send-off than I was.

"Thank you very much for your time, Mr. Carey,"

he said. "I'll see you at the police station with your lawyer."

On the way back to Revere, I took the Hurley folder out of my briefcase to insert my new notes.

"I had a few more questions," I said, "but I guess they'll have to wait."

"You did all right with the time you had," Matt said. "Those numbers you had at the tip of your fingers—very impressive."

"I just learned them this morning," I said, reverting to my old-time habit of self-effacement. "The numbers are on the Internet."

"Maybe, but not everyone knows how to get them or what they mean."

"So, do you think he did it?" I asked, amazed at my ability to change a subject.

"I'm not ruling him out."

Before I closed my Hurley folder, I made a neat pile of the newspaper clippings from the day following the murder. A headline caught my eye and I remembered something I'd wanted to ask Matt.

"One of these clips says that the 911 call came in shortly after eight o'clock on Sunday night," I said.

"Right. Mrs. Whitestone was at the back of the house, without her hearing aids, and didn't hear anything. The young couple next door heard a loud noise and the screech of a car leaving in a hurry. They went out to check and called 911."

"But another clip here says that Hurley died late

Sunday night. Eight o'clock isn't 'late.' Did Hurley live for a while in the hospital?"

"She did. She hung on for a couple of hours, but didn't regain consciousness."

"Did she say anything at all? Maybe to the people who found her or the paramedics?"

"You sound like Mrs. Whitestone. She demanded to talk to all the people who handled Margaret, asking how she was and if she had any last words."

"Did she?"

"As a matter of fact, the paramedic has her making some sound. I can't quite remember, but I wrote it down. If you want to reach into my coat pocket on the backseat, you can take out my notebook."

I leaned over and pulled Matt's coat toward me. I found his notebook and flipped through some pages, stopping at one headed *Paramedic*. I was impressed with his organizational skills and legible handwriting. *The sign of a good researcher*, I thought, *if someone else can follow your notes.*

"It looks like 'mole,' " I said. "As in 'spy'?"

"That's what the guy said. Mole or moles. No name in the case sounds like that, so I gave up on it as a lead. And, of course, she kept asking for Mrs. Whitestone. That's it."

"Hmm," was all I said, but something else that I couldn't put my finger on was churning in my brain.

Chapter Twelve

Trying to cultivate at least one healthy habit, on the way home I stopped at a market and picked up bread and fruit and raw material for a salad. At the last minute, I added a quart of ice cream to my basket, unable to resist a new Ben & Jerry's flavor with caramel and marshmallows. *For unexpected company*, I told myself.

Mrs. Whitestone had chosen the old custom—two evenings of wake before burial—so Wednesday evening presented another opportunity to talk to the principals in the case.

I had to weigh my desire to meet Patrick Gallagher and Vincent Cavallo against the dread of encountering Rocky Busso again. I threw the probability of seeing Matt into the equation, although he hadn't said anything about attending the wake. All in all, I entertained one final vision of Rocky's tiny eyes and puffy face

106

and came down on the side of staying in my apartment.

"I have too much to do tonight," I said, talking to Rose over the intercom.

"I'll stop by when we're finished and give you any news," she said. "Don't forget, the cruiser will be out there again tonight."

Following my theory of no personal attacks while a police car is outside one's door and Christmas music is playing, I put on a CD of *The Messiah*. I changed into comfortable pants and a loose black sweater and went to my computer. I checked my e-mail, paid some bills, and opened my Hurley file. After typing in the new notes from the interview with Carey, I printed out the whole file and took the pages, with a cup of coffee, to my rocker.

Somehow, I'd convinced Matt to let me make photocopies of the letters in Hurley's personal correspondence file, and I added those to the pile of paper on my lap. I sat back and glided a few minutes on my rocker, enjoying the music. It was a nice reminder that my weekend was looking good.

I sorted through my notes, Hurley's letters, and the newspaper clippings, looking for a pattern or an indisputable clue to Hurley's murderer. I was amazed at my own arrogance—did I really believe I could solve this high-profile murder more easily or quickly than all of the police power of Revere and the neighboring cities that had been brought in for support? Did I care so much about justice in general, and Congresswoman Margaret Hurley in particular?

Was I trying to impress Sgt. Matt Gennaro? Or did I just love a puzzle? I settled on ''all of the above,'' and got to work.

I reviewed what I knew about each suspect—William Carey, Patrick Gallagher, Buddy Hurley, and Vincent Cavallo had all made my list, in that order. I'd moved Carey into first place after meeting him—realizing that assigning guilt by familiarity probably wouldn't make it in the annals of detective work.

Buddy's alibi was the most solid, witnessed by a large crowd in a public place, but I didn't think it meant much, since it wouldn't have been hard for him to hire someone to do the deed. I flashed on an image of Buddy Hurley handing over a thick envelope to Rocky Busso, both nodding knowingly. And I didn't doubt that Carey had access to a large pool of very strong cowboys.

Since alibis were a dispensable variable in my theory of the case, I moved on to clues, which were as scarce as women in physics. The only real clue in my mind was Margaret Hurley's last word, or syllable, before she died.

I made a list of all the possible meanings of ''mo'' or ''mole.'' I ruled out a license plate since I couldn't imagine anyone's using a car with vanity plates as a murder weapon. I doubted that Hurley meant mole/ spy, since there was no national security issue that I was aware of with the helium reserves. Did the murderer have a mole on his body? I deemed it impossible that Hurley would have been able to see a mole on the driver of a vehicle coming at her full speed, in the dark. Or that a gopherlike, furry underground animal was behind the wheel.

Leaving alibis and clues for a while, I focused on motive. Although Buddy had been written out of his father's will, I was sure that more options opened up to him with Margaret out of the way. Maybe the courts would look more kindly on a sole heir. On the "not so nice" side of the ledger for his sister was renewed gossip that it was Margaret who had instigated the change of will not long before both parents died in a plane crash.

I was neither proud nor completely trusting of my sources for these tidbits—TV coverage, news magazines, and hearsay from Rose the Eavesdropper—but not much was forthcoming from Matt the Detective on nontechnical matters.

The motive I'd assigned to Cavallo was different from the others. It didn't have to do with either love or money, but professional reputation and frustration. Weak, I concluded, so he was my last choice. The only strange thing was why Margaret Hurley had put Cavallo's letters in her personal file. From what I'd read, everything he'd said in the letters was already in his public reports, the ones I'd found on the Internet.

Matt had invited me to Cavallo's interview the next afternoon, Thursday, but not to Gallagher's or Buddy's in the morning. They had no apparent link to the helium program, so there was no technical reason for me to be there. *Maybe on our Saturday date I'll speak to Matt about this handicap he's giv-*

ing me, I thought, *and also find out what he's done about Al's notebook;* but I doubted it. I knew I'd be concentrating on not tripping on Boston's cobblestone streets.

I'd had only a brief glimpse of Gallagher, plus copies of two letters he'd written to Hurley, plus Rose's account of his drunken apology to the victim; so far, not exactly winning behavior. I'd had even less direct contact with Buddy, if you didn't count the intensity of the moment I did have with him.

I wanted to talk to Gallagher and Buddy so badly that I reconsidered going downstairs to the wake, and probably would have, if I hadn't changed out of my professional mortuary clothing and misplaced the staff ribbon that provided a modicum of armor.

I took another glance at the piece about Gallagher in the newspaper and let out a tiny gasp when I read that he worked for the school district and had an office at Revere High School. *How did I miss that before?* I wondered, with mounting excitement. *And what's the protocol for asking one's ex-boyfriend to introduce her to a murder suspect?*

Before I could change my mind, I picked up the phone and called Peter. I owed him a call, anyway, I reasoned, and maybe I could trade Christmas lunch for an introduction. Or maybe Peter knew Gallagher well and we could all go to lunch, I thought, pushing positive thinking way over the limit.

Peter answered, with the voice of one who has just swallowed a bite of dinner.

"I'm sorry to call you at dinnertime," I told him.

"Not at all. I'm delighted, Gloria. I was wondering if you got my message the other night."

"I did. I've been busy, working on your class, too, of course." I was disgusted with my fawning, but I did need his help to carry out my limited duties for the RPD.

"I'm looking forward to Monday," Peter said. "All I ever wanted to know about Marconi, right? And I'm hoping you're free for lunch afterward. We need to do Christmas."

I shivered at the thought of getting close to someone who "did Christmas," but I persevered.

"I'll count on lunch," I said.

I managed a few more sentences of chit-chat about Peter's plans for the holidays and the state of health of his sister, his nephews, and grand-nephews, then got to the point.

"By the way, Peter," I asked, "do you know Patrick Gallagher?"

"Not well. I work with him a little, since he's running our curriculum project for the district. He keeps an office in our building." As Peter progressed through his sentences, his voice became softer and his speech slower until, finally, he ended with a long, heavy sigh, and I knew he'd put the pieces of my call together. "Gloria," he said.

"I'd like to meet him, Peter, just briefly."

"And that's why you're calling?" It was more a statement than a question, and I couldn't argue with it. My silence must have said as much, so Peter continued.

"Gloria, I don't know what bothers me more, that you're way over your head investigating a murder on your own, or that you're using me to do it."

"Peter, I don't need you to do my job. And let me remind you that this victim is our representative to the United States Congress, yours and mine."

"It's tragic, Gloria, but it's not your job."

"I'm simply asking you for a favor that you're obviously not willing to do. Let's forget the idea, Peter. I'm sorry I bothered you and I'll see you on Monday for class."

"Wait," Peter said. "I know how stubborn you are, and you'll get what you want one way or another. I can take you down to Gallagher's office. I have to drop some papers off to him anyway."

I ignored the slur on my character and took what I could get.

"Thanks, Peter," I said. "When?"

"Tomorrow morning, early, say, eight-thirty. He's not going to be here after nine."

I almost said, "I know," remembering Matt's interview schedule. I had a few qualms about talking to Gallagher even before Matt did, but I shrugged them off.

"I'll meet you in the main office, where I usually do," I said. "Eight-thirty. Can I bring you a coffee?"

"Decaf," Peter said, and we hung up.

Just after nine, Rose and Frank came upstairs, looking as exhausted as I'd ever seen them. I actually detected wrinkles in Rose's navy blue knit suit, and Frank's eyes were half closed.

I insisted that they relax while I brought them drinks—wine for Rose and a beer for Frank. Since I never drank alcohol, my entire liquor collection consisted of what others, including the two of them, had brought into my apartment at one time or another. I made coffee for myself and sat across from them.

"You missed a big night," Rose said. "I think the whole Democratic side of the aisle was there, and a few Republicans, too. And this is the first time we've had a Kennedy in our parlor—young Joseph—isn't it, Frank?"

From Rose's lips, it sounded as though royalty had come to tea in their home. Since coming back to Revere, I'd noticed that the Kennedys still held magic for natives of Massachusetts. After so many years on the West Coast, I'd forgotten the enduring charm of Camelot.

"I think so," Frank said. "We thought Teddy might come for the bishop last year, but he apparently couldn't." Frank removed his jacket and placed it carefully around the curved dark wood of the chair at my desk, then sat back and closed his eyes.

"So, what's new," I asked Rose, folding my hands on my lap, "besides the congresspeople?"

"He wasn't there, just his partner."

"He? You mean Matt? That's not all I want to know about."

"It should be," Rose said, but her smile softened the reproach. She sipped her wine and continued. "No scenes tonight. The brother and his muscle were there. Gallagher wasn't. I'm sorry, I didn't pick up a thing. It was so crowded every minute. Robert and the boys are still down there straightening up.''

I felt very guilty pumping my friend for information when she'd worked so hard and all I'd done was read my notes and manipulate Peter into doing me a favor.

''Thanks anyway,'' I said, moving the bowl of cashews closer to her.

''So what about Saturday night?'' Rose said, but without the spirit I expected. ''The funeral's tomorrow, so maybe we can go shopping on Friday and get you a new outfit.'' She stifled a yawn as Frank slept beside her, snoring gently.

''Let's talk about it tomorrow,'' I said. ''I'm not even sure you're all right to drive home. You're both exhausted and the streets are still icy.''

''Robert's going to drive us. But I guess you're right. We'd better go down and gather our things.''

I walked my friends to the door and let them out, disappointed on many counts—I had nothing new to think about, no company for the rest of the evening, and no fun conversation about Saturday's plans.

As I cleared the glasses and napkins, I noticed that Frank had left his jacket on my chair. I was considering whether to race downstairs with it, when I heard a knock.

I picked up the jacket and opened the door.

Rocky Busso was standing on my threshold.

Chapter Thirteen

I felt my heart beating against my throat, and my knees went weak. I squinted, opened my mouth, and tilted my head to the side, as if I'd just seen an unexpected glitch in a curve on my oscilloscope.

"Dr. Lamerino," Rocky said, bowing slightly from the waist. "Can I come in?"

He held his hat in his hands in front of him, giving him a meek and humble look. Either that, or he was hiding his gun, I thought. The moment was like a dream—in my mind I reacted quickly, slamming the door in his face before he could move a muscle, but my body was absolutely rigid, my arms stiff as meter sticks.

If Rocky sensed my fear, he gave no indication. He might have been a Boy Scout selling cookies, or whatever little male scouts did for a living.

I stepped aside, taking a few steps backward into

my living room, under the spell of my own panic. Rocky entered my apartment and walked past me, as far as my couch. He'd switched his hat to one hand and I saw that there was no gun, at least none aimed at me. So far, he'd said only six words, but his presence was overwhelming. His enormous bulk, spread mostly in the horizontal direction, seemed to raise the temperature of my apartment, and his sharp-smelling cologne saturated my nostrils.

Rocky was standing between me and my window, and I couldn't figure out how to get past him to where I could see if the cruiser was still parked on Tuttle Street. Another thing that worried me was that the Christmas disc had ended, leaving me very vulnerable.

With the speed of a Pentium processor, I raced through the pros and cons of my options. Number one, run out the door and down the steps—useless if he had a gun, or a backup team waiting on the landing. Number two, scream at the top of my lungs—futile if no one was in the building, and probably aggravating to Rocky. I didn't want to aggravate Rocky. Number three, attack Rocky—and bounce back from the shiny buttons of his expensive-looking black wool coat.

During this lightning-speed calculation, my body had remained essentially immobile, and in the end, I did what I always do. I chose the intellectual approach.

"How do you know me?" I asked, as evenly as I could, finally articulating the question that had been in the back of my mind all day.

"You're Al Gravese's girlfriend," Rocky said, answering the wrong question.

"Did you know Al?" I asked.

"I worked for Al. I was just a kid," he said, smoothing down his ample head of black-and-gray hair.

In spite of his heavyweight physique, Rocky's manner was so gentle that I almost offered to take his coat and invite him to sit down. "Did you like your job?" I might ask, over an espresso.

"What can I do for you?" was what I actually asked, as if I were in charge.

"We know you're digging into Al's accident. Don't do that."

"How . . . ?"

"We knew you was back in town," Rocky said, not disappointing me with his grammatical deviations. "We always thought you was too smart for Al." At this, Rocky chuckled and bowed from the waist again. "And now you're a doctor."

I figured Rocky thought "doctor" meant I could fix broken bones, and I hoped he hadn't come to recruit me. Although he'd given me no cause for alarm, I stayed in my no-risk, no-tricky-questions mode.

"I don't think I've ever met you," I said.

"We kept to ourselves," he said. "I came to tell you there's no way to track down thirty-four-year-old business. They're almost all dead now. And all you need to know is Al did a little too much drinking that night and he went off the road."

"Who—?"

Rocky interrupted again, and I was starting to resent my one-syllable allotment.

"Al was crazy about you," he said. "Before he left the club that night, he gave me an errand to do." Rocky reached into his pocket, causing an involuntary gasp to leave my throat. To my great relief, he pulled out an item too small to be a weapon, and handed it to me—a small red velvet box, discolored and worn with age. "I picked this up for him at that jeweler's on Broadway."

I opened the box and saw an enormous diamond ring, at least nine millimeters in diameter, and equally deep in its setting. On the inside diameter was the inscription "AG♥GL."

"I already had an engagement ring," I said, as if I were rejecting a proposal from Rocky himself.

"That one was kind of cheap, you know. Al came into some money and wanted to get you a really good one. This one's two carats," he said as proudly as if he'd bought it. "He was going to give it to you Christmas Eve."

"And you've kept it all these years?" I had the ring in one hand and the box in the other, feeling like I was at the controls of a time machine.

"Tell you the truth," Rocky said, "I almost used it a couple of times, but I figured it would be *malocchio*, you know, a curse. I mean, it was supposed to go to you."

"Thank you, Rocky," I said, finally gesturing toward a seat. *Surely he wouldn't give me a ring, then blow me away,* I thought.

Rocky refused my offer and was walking toward the door, his thirty-four-year-old errand brought to closure. But I wasn't quite finished with him. Although I wasn't anxious to pursue the topic of Al Gravese, and I had no idea what to do with a large diamond ring, I did have some pressing questions about a present-day investigation.

"Do you know anything about Margaret Hurley's murder?" I asked, certain that I'd lost all common sense.

Rocky didn't blink an eye.

"Don't go there," he said, and headed for the door—where, for the second surprise of the evening, I saw Sgt. Matt Gennaro.

Where were you when I thought I needed you? I almost said.

Rocky nodded to me and to Matt, put his hat on, and walked out into the hallway and down the stairs. I watched his exit and Matt's appearance like a stage director who'd lost control of his cast.

Once I was able to focus my attention on Matt, I rushed to my own defense.

"I didn't invite him," I said. I had a vivid memory of the time last fall when Matt stormed around my apartment, angry at me, just because I'd been entertaining all the suspects in a murder investigation in my apartment.

"I know that," he said, with a smile that comforted me. I let out a long sigh, the accumulation of more than twenty-four hours of pent-up anxiety, starting when I'd heard Rocky utter my name on the first evening of the wake.

"You knew he was up here?"

"I saw him put Buddy in a car, then reenter the building and go up the stairs."

"I thought you weren't here tonight. And why didn't you stop him?" *And why don't I just bang my fists on the table?* I thought, aware of my shrill voice.

"I've been here all evening," he said, "outside in an unmarked, and walking around the property. I guess your sources aren't that keen." He had a delightful, teasing twinkle in his eyes, and I lifted my arms in embarrassed defeat. "Secondly," he continued, "I wasn't worried because I knew he knew—he saw the cruiser with the uniforms outside; he saw me follow him into the building and watch him climb the stairs, if you understand what I'm saying."

I understood.

"You're not a good liar, directly or indirectly," Matt said. "I knew you'd started going through Al's book, so I was keeping an eye out, but I thought I'd give you a few minutes with Busso."

I was still holding the ring and the box, and saw Matt glance down at them.

"He came to give me my engagement ring," I said, sounding like the college girl I was the first time I'd received a diamond.

Matt nodded as if he knew about the ring, but I suspected that he just couldn't come up with an appropriate response. *Who could?* I asked myself.

We were still standing close to the door. Matt rubbed his hands together and blew on them. "Do you think I could have a cup of coffee?" he asked. "I'm freezing."

Matt's request woke me out of my semitrance, and it came to me that I'd been more hospitable to Rocky than to Matt. An image of Josephine came to my mind, and I rushed to the kitchen, putting the ring, now resting in its cushioned box, on the counter.

I gave Matt coffee and a plate of snacks since, by his admission, he'd eaten only "stakeout food" that evening.

I sat on my rocker, across from him, and gave him a full account of my conversation with Rocky.

"I learned a lot in a few minutes," I said. "I came face-to-face with Al's connections, you might say."

"Are you all right with this, Gloria?"

"I am. It might take a while to process everything."

"Give yourself time." Matt was sitting on the edge of my couch, leaning forward, his face showing concern.

"I guess he was telling me that Al was set up to be killed, but the ones responsible are all dead, or almost all dead, and, anyway, I think I'm through with this."

"So you're not going to hit me up for a copy of the notebook?"

"No," I said, probably taking him more seriously than he intended. "I still have some questions, of course, like what had Al done to deserve being killed, and is anyone else in that book besides Rocky alive today. But I'm definitely ready to file this away."

As I rambled, I sipped my coffee and stared past Matt, at the tops of the snowy trees outside my window. A streetlight in front of the building cast a yellowish glow over my white drapes, and I imagined I was looking at a very old photograph.

Matt drained his cup and stood to leave. I realized I'd lost track of his presence.

"I'm going to be on my way," he said. "I'll see you tomorrow afternoon."

"Right," I said, as if I'd been thinking of Vincent Cavallo and his helium report all along. "One o'clock."

"And, best of all, I'll see you Saturday evening," he said.

"I'm really looking forward to that, too."

I smiled, but Matt's comment didn't have half the effect it would have under different circumstances.

"Be good to yourself, Gloria," Matt said, giving me a brief, one-armed hug as he walked past me out the door.

I went back to my rocker, with no inclination either to sleep or to do anything useful. I rubbed my ring finger as if to awaken more memories, or to put order into the ones I had. I drifted far away, back to 1962.

I'm with Al Gravese, at a flower show. I don't especially like attending flower shows, but it's one of Al's passions, and I'm happy to be his date. I'm bored by the talks on the latest in mulch or crossbreeding tulips, and all the different breeds of orchids look alike to me, but I smile a lot and fix my hair and make sure my lipstick is even.

I'm fishing with Al Gravese. I hate being out on the water in a small boat, and I can't stand the sight of worms or the smell of dead fish, but I laugh and snap Al's picture and say what fun it is.

I'm at a baseball game with Al Gravese and his buddies. I'd rather be at the museum or a concert, but I eat hot dogs and yell at the umpire, and cheer when the Red Sox score a run.

Al was crazy about the girl on his arm, I thought, but Al didn't know me any more than I knew him.

I turned out the lights in the living room, and went in to sleep.

Chapter Fourteen

I noticed more activity than usual for a weekday in front of St. Anthony's Church as I left my building on Thursday morning, December 8, the Feast of the Immaculate Conception. I recalled a time when I believed that an eternal pit of fire awaited those who missed mass on this day. I wondered if the parishioners filing into church in the 1990s believed that, and I also wondered exactly what I believed now.

On the way to my meeting with Peter and Patrick Gallagher I made a detour to a small coffee shop on Beach Street. It was a new café, with modern furniture and espresso machines, but its freshly painted walls were covered with old photographs of Revere Beach in its heyday. In spite of the frigid morning air outside and the Christmas music inside, I was brought back to hot, humid summer days as I walked around and studied the enlarged black-and-white snapshots—a pony diving from a forty-foot platform into a tank of water on the Boulevard, shapely young women in modest black swimsuits lined up for a bathing beauty contest, a man shot from a cannon, flying one hundred feet into the sky.

At the table next to mine was a young mother and her daughter, wearing nearly identical pink quilted nylon jackets. As I sipped espresso through a thick layer of foam, I watched them out of the corner of my eye. They worked together on a page in a coloring book, giggling over a silly picture, their matching blond hair falling onto their work. I could smell the little girl's hot chocolate and wished I could tell her how lucky she was.

As hard as I'd tried over the years, I could never remember a time when Josephine and I laughed together, or even colored together. I was sure that her own Depression-era youth held few joys, and I tried to forgive her for not recovering in time to give me a childhood. It's never too late for a happy childhood, pop psychologists claimed, but I was too busy working on a happy adulthood.

The Revere High School building was brand new, as far as I was concerned, having been built long after I'd left for California. I met Peter in the main office, where I signed a clipboard at the reception desk. His mood was about as cool as his crisp white shirt, but he warmed up a bit when I gave him a steaming decaf mocha, a bag of biscotti, and an outline for six more guest appearances in his class.

We went to the faculty lounge, a surprisingly ample room with a couch along one wall and a kitchen area with a few tables and chairs. I wondered if Peter, a confirmed antitechnologist, ever used the minisized white microwave oven on the counter.

"I asked Gallagher to meet me here around eight-thirty," Peter said, as he snapped off a piece of biscotti. "I thought it would be less awkward than dragging you down to his office."

"That was really a good idea, Peter," I said, meaning every word. I'd spent a good part of my time in the shower that morning wondering just how I would manage an interview with Gallagher, standing at the threshold of his office. A conversation seemed much more feasible if we were sitting around a table in the lounge, but I still didn't know precisely what approach to take, except that I wished I'd brought him a mocha.

"How shall I introduce you?" Peter asked, causing me to feel like a criminal who carried multiple passports with different identities. I had a moment of longing for my years as a simple physicist wearing a white lab coat over whatever outfit was clean that day.

It took me a while to answer Peter's question. Not knowing whether I should represent myself as a Galigani Mortuary staff person or a Revere Police Department consultant, I'd chosen clothing befitting either occupation—a black rayon suit with an ivory silk blouse and a long string of pearls. I wore a small round pin on my lapel, with the official logo of an undergraduate physics group I'd been adviser to. Its dull green background featured a miniature schematic in gold, showing waves leaving a moving source, also known as the Doppler effect.

"Just introduce me as your friend, I think," I told Peter, having decided that I might learn more in a casual interaction than in a formal capacity, not that I really had a formal capacity, I reminded myself.

Patrick Gallagher came into the lounge only seconds after I'd determined who I'd be for the morning. He presented a striking picture, with his wavy red hair, dark blue suit, and polished black oxfords. Only the redness around his eyes and his tired breathing gave away the emotional strain I imagined he was under. Otherwise, I had no trouble imagining him fitting well in the social circles of Washington and wondered what had driven him and Congresswoman Hurley apart.

Gallagher took Peter's folder, hardly acknowledging his words of introduction. He seemed in a hurry to leave, so I made a frenzied attempt to engage him in conversation.

"I'm so sorry about the death of your friend, Margaret Hurley," I said to him. "Are you going to attend the funeral this morning?"

"No, I can't make it."

I knew that Matt wouldn't have scheduled an interview unless Gallagher had already decided to stay away from the services.

"I suppose it would very hard on you," I said.

Gallagher looked at me with curiosity, finally making eye contact. A side glance gave me a view of Peter, who put his elbows on the table, hands at his forehead, as if he couldn't bear to watch.

"Yes," Gallagher said, half turning to leave the lounge.

"I happen to live in the apartment upstairs from Galigani's Mortuary," I said, "and I know how difficult this week has been for you."

Gallagher shook his head, a pained expression on his face.

"And your concern in all this is?"

I was greatly distressed at how the meeting was going, realizing that Matt was right to keep me out of nontechnical interviews. I didn't have a clue how to proceed, and I'd obviously upset Gallagher.

Peter had gone over to the kitchen area, taking an inordinately long time to throw away his plastic cup and napkins and wash his hands.

"I'm sorry," I told Gallagher. "I didn't mean to pry." But of course I did; I just didn't know how to be cool about it. "I'm working on a report for the police department," I said, pulling a second identity out of my hat.

"You're a cop?"

"No, I . . ."

"Then I don't have to talk to you, do I?"

"No, you don't."

"Is there any reason you followed me to work today?"

I had no good response for this, not wanting to implicate Peter in what was turning out to be one of the worst ideas I'd ever had. However, a glance at Peter, standing at the sink with his arms folded across his chest, told me that I had nothing more to lose.

"Have you been able to find someone who saw you at the Northgate mall on the evening of Ms. Hurley's murder?" I asked.

Gallagher's face looked ready to explode as his nostrils flared and his eyes bulged. For once I felt that my age, short stature, and gender served me well. I had a strong feeling that if I were young, tall, male, or any of the above, Patrick Gallagher would have punched me in the nose.

Instead he took a deep breath, turned away from me, and nodded at Peter.

"You'll have to excuse me," he said, not as an apology, but as a loud parting statement as he left the room.

I was sure my face was red. Not only had I brought stress to someone who might not deserve it, but I'd given Peter an excellent demonstration of how poor a detective I really was. And maybe I'd also spoiled his relationship with Patrick Gallagher, with whom he had to work. I couldn't bear to look up from my biscotti crumbs.

"Peter," I said, "I'm sorry I put you through this."

"I am, too."

"I'll understand if you prefer to cancel Monday's class or lunch or both."

"I have a class at nine," he said, and left the lounge.

I left the building and drove directly home, hoping I wouldn't run into anyone I knew. Fortunately, that was unlikely—I hadn't made many friends since moving back to Revere. It was one skill I'd never developed, and I couldn't help thinking I'd be better at it if Josephine had taken me to a coffee shop once in a while when I was a little girl, and colored and giggled with me.

Just before I turned down Tuttle Street, I saw the long line of funeral cars coming from St. Anthony's parking lot. One flower car after another made its way down the street, with more floral arrangements than the biggest shows I'd been to at Horticultural Hall with Al.

Although I couldn't see her, I envisioned a stoic Frances Whitestone in the first car, suffering in silence, keeping her shoulders back and refusing offers of assistance. I pulled over as the procession passed, and bowed my head, clutching the steering wheel of my luxury car as if it were the top of a prie-dieu.

I felt worse than ever about my inability to accomplish anything positive in the course of the investigation into Margaret Hurley's death. I dismissed the idea that there was some connection between my failed interview with Gallagher and missing mass on a Holy Day of Obligation.

By the time I reached my apartment, I was in a mood that only food and work could help, so I dived into both. Rejecting my first inclination, ice cream at nine-thirty in the morning, I settled for a grilled cheese and coffee.

With Cavallo's reports and letters spread out on my table, I ate my brunch and looked for a clue as to why the two letters were in Hurley's personal file. And, I admitted to myself, for some way to redeem my poor performance thus far.

After an hour of staring at Cavallo's list of proposals for improving the operations of the helium facility, I practically knew them from memory. I was about to give up, except for one tiny idea left in the back of my mind.

I went to my computer and called up the home page for the helium facility. After waiting several minutes for the elaborate graphics to download, I was able to click on a link to the operation's contractors. Sure enough, in the fine print, I saw the name, Vincent Cavallo, private consultant.

"Aha," I said to my empty flat, and felt I deserved a nap.

Two hours later, I sat outside Matt's office, refreshed and ready with my Internet scoop—yet another conflict of interest in the Hurley case. A young woman in a starched white shirt with an RPD patch on her sleeve had told me that Matt was at lunch. She offered me coffee, but I'd chosen to keep my private vow never to drink office brew.

I was looking through my notes when Matt appeared, about ten minutes before one.

"Did you sleep all right?" he asked, looking like he hadn't had the luxury of a nap.

"Revisiting 1962 wasn't exactly conducive to rest," I said, "but I've made up for it. I guess I wasn't very good company last night."

"You're always good company," he said, in keeping with our backdoor way of flirting with each other. I didn't deliberately plan these entries into compliments, and I don't think Matt did either; it seemed just the natural course of awkward, middle-aged courtship. I wondered when we'd be comfortable and confident enough to address our feelings directly—assuming he *had* any feelings for me, Josephine's voice reminded me.

I wasn't sure what time Cavallo was due, so I got to business quickly, telling Matt about the new conflict of interest I'd discovered.

I thought it was about time for a verbal pat on the back, when we were interrupted by a ringing phone. Matt picked up the receiver and gave only brief responses to the party on the other end, writing in his notebook all the while.

"When?" I heard him say, and then "where," and "how," and "what," until I thought I was listening in on a journalism class. When he hung up, his expression was serious, his tone very low.

"Rocky Busso was found dead an hour ago," he said. "An apparent suicide. He left a note confessing to Hurley's murder."

Chapter Fifteen

I felt a shiver through my whole body, and a sadness that surprised me. I couldn't believe that Rocky Busso was dead, and I couldn't believe that I cared. I also felt waves of doubt—that he took his own life, or that he was solely responsible for Hurley's murder—all the more amazing considering how fearful I'd been of him. It seemed that the few minutes he'd spent in my apartment changed my view of him completely, and I felt closer to this victim than to Congresswoman Hurley.

From the distance created by my mental wanderings, I heard Matt's voice.

"Gloria?"

He gave me a look I'd come to recognize as concern—his brow knotted into wrinkles, his mouth twisted a little to the left.

"I'm shocked," I said. "Do you really think there's anything to it?"

"That he's dead?"

"That he did it himself, or that he murdered Hurley?"

"It does have a funny ring to it. It's not usually that simple," Matt said, talking as much to himself as to me. "We'll certainly be looking into it. It's not your problem, though, is it?"

"I think he was hired to kill her, but whoever was supposed to pay him, killed him instead." My declaration came out with much more emotion than I'd planned, and I realized I'd snapped a red plastic paper clip in two while I was talking. "Maybe he wanted more money or something, or maybe he wanted out of the life," I said.

"Evidently Rocky's good deed had a greater effect on you than you thought. Are you going to be all right? You've had a lot to deal with this week, Gloria, and I think you should call it quits for a while."

"I wonder if he told any of his friends he was expecting money, or . . ."

"You're not listening, are you?"

"I'm afraid of what you're going to say."

"Like, 'you're off the case?' "

"Something like that. You know I can't drop things, Matt. Cavallo will be here any minute, and you'll need me," I said, waving my notes in the air to emphasize my point.

As if by some magic, coincident with the fluttering papers, a uniformed officer appeared in the doorway with Vincent Cavallo, much younger and much more handsome than I'd pictured, with dark hair and eyes and a nose so perfect I knew he couldn't be all Italian. Was it my imagination, or were they giving Ph.D.s out sooner than they used to, I wondered, and to better-looking people?

I knew it would be awkward for Matt to fire me in front of company, so I used the occasion to my advantage.

"You have some very interesting proposals," I said to Cavallo, immediately after Matt introduced me. "I'm especially curious about the idea of eliminating cylinder-filling but increasing sales of crude helium."

There, I thought, *he can't fire me now.*

Matt gave me a side glance and shook his head. I knew I hadn't heard the last of his worries, but at least for the duration of this interview I was safe from downsizing.

Cavallo answered three or four questions I had, laying out the statistics on the balance of revenues, and when he was relaxed and confident, Matt stepped in.

"Tell me about your association with the federal helium operations," he said.

Cavallo shifted in his seat, placing both feet on the floor in front of him. He unbuttoned his leather jacket and loosened the scarf around his neck. I was most disappointed when he screwed up his mouth and disturbed his poster-boy features.

"I'm not associated with the helium facility," he said.

"You're listed as a private consultant."

"I'm not representing myself in that regard."

"I don't understand," Matt said. "Do you or don't you receive contracts and money from the helium facility?"

"In a way."

"In a way," Matt said, clicking his tongue. "And haven't you also received money to evaluate the facility as an independent expert, as if you had no interest in it?"

Cavallo's smooth, low baritone had changed to one slightly higher in pitch, and I noticed that he'd begun to play with his watchband. I felt like part of an experimental psychology team, where I set up the subjects and Matt came in with the "gotcha" questions.

"I receive contracts, but I'm not the endpoint. I represent another party who has the controlling interest in what I do." Cavallo spoke with seconds, if not minutes, between words, as if he were making his way slowly through a test in a foreign language.

Matt, on the other hand, came through quickly and to the point.

"Controlling interest in a private consulting firm? Are you saying you have an anonymous partner?"

"Yes, you could say that."

"No one stays anonymous for very long in a murder investigation, Mr. Cavallo," Matt said. "Who is your partner?"

"I can't tell you that."

Matt sighed and put his pencil down on his desk.

"All right, Mr. Cavallo, but you know we'll get this

information sooner or later, and your cooperation would mean a lot here."

Cavallo gulped, and I thought I saw perspiration on his forehead.

"I'm going to have to check things out first."

Matt stood up, and Cavallo followed suit.

"I have one other question for you, Mr. Cavallo," I said. "Does the nickname 'mole' mean anything to you?"

Cavallo ran his tongue over his teeth and shook his head.

"No," he said, "it doesn't. Sorry."

Matt looked at me and scratched his neck, then addressed Cavallo.

"We'll be in touch," Matt told him.

Cavallo left the office without another word.

"Mole?" Matt said. "You still think that's a clue, don't you?"

"I do, and as for Cavallo, I think he's shady, and I'm embarrassed that he's a physicist, but I don't think he's a killer."

Matt sat down, and it seemed we were going to pick up where we were before Cavallo's interview, when I'd almost lost my job. I tried a preemptive strategy.

"What exactly did Busso's confession say?" I asked him.

"Of course, I haven't seen it," he said, apparently caught off guard by my tactic, "but he did know some details about the murder that we haven't released to the press or to anyone else, for that matter." He leafed through his notebook and, to my amazement, continued feeding me information. "He wrote something about Hurley's garment bag and flashlight."

"Flashlight?"

"She was holding a flashlight in one hand and her garment bag in the other when she was found."

"She was holding a flashlight? So she could have seen something?"

"It was just a small one, like the kind you'd carry on your key ring."

"Still," I said, while some neurons traveled through my head, unable to find the connection they knew they should make.

"And that about wraps it up, Gloria," Matt said. "I can't think of a single other thing I'll be needing you for before Saturday night."

He came around to my side of his desk and, smiling, put his arms on my shoulders and spun me around toward the door. It was the most playful gesture he'd ever made, and because of that, I didn't mind leaving.

I knew better than to take Matt's light tone in ushering me from his office as a sign that he was willing to have me continue working on the case. But I couldn't stop thinking about the pieces of the investigation, even after I got home.

Around four o'clock, I made coffee, put on a CD of Christmas hymns sung by the Mormon Tabernacle Choir, and brought one of my rockers close to the window. I left my apartment lights off and watched the darkness move in on the beautiful elms of Tuttle Street.

Christmas lights came on, as far as I could see, up and down the street, but the music and lights were no longer enough to give me a feeling of security. What had I been thinking? I asked myself. Hadn't Al died four days before Christmas? And now Margaret Hurley and Rocky Busso were struck down amid sleigh bells and cheerful wrapping paper.

I felt a chill as I acknowledged that murder doesn't take a holiday. I turned on my lights and took out my notes.

I didn't for a minute believe that the powerful man who'd delivered my engagement ring had taken his own life. I thought it strange that it was easier for me to accept Rocky as the murderer of Margaret Hurley than of himself.

Since I'd had at least a few minutes with Gallagher and Cavallo, the only unknown left was Buddy Hurley. I needed to find out more about him. But there was no technical connection, and I didn't relish Matt's finding out that I'd dropped in on a chief suspect. Eventually, another, more reasonable plan took shape in my mind.

How, I asked myself, *do writers come up with long articles about celebrities, even when they refuse to be interviewed? The way they do it,* I answered myself, *is the way detectives "interview" dead people—they talk to friends, relatives, neighbors. At last,* I thought, mentally hitting my forehead with the palm of my hand, *I'm catching on to police work.*

I picked up my copy of the Revere telephone directory, and opened to Whitestone. I found several, but no Frances, and the only F. Whitestone was not on Oxford Park. It made sense that Frances Whitestone would have an unlisted telephone number. It also made sense that the funeral director in charge of her friend's services would have that number.

Pushing aside the memory of my fiasco with the Peter Mastrone/Patrick Gallagher combination, I prepared myself to extract a favor from another friend.

I knew that Rose and Frank had planned to go home after the funeral in the morning, and I resisted bothering them after their grueling week. My obsession with the Hurley case propelled me forward, however, and I picked up my telephone and punched in the Galiganis' number. Instead of the build-up-and-manipulate scheme I'd used on Peter, I chose the direct approach with Rose.

"Rose," I said, when I heard her voice, "I need a favor."

"Sure, what's up?"

"I need Frances Whitestone's telephone number."

"The old lady?" Rose asked, stifling a yawn.

"The old lady," I said, carrying my cordless phone to my window. With my free hand, I pulled the drapes to rid myself of my reflection, which I saw as that of the worst kind of person, taking advantage of my best friend's weakened condition. "How did she hold up this morning, by the way?"

"Like a rock. She's an amazing woman. Why do you want her number?"

Oh-oh, I thought. *Rose is starting to wake up; time to move fast.*

"Gloria?" This time her voice was suspicious, and I knew I'd been found out.

"If it's in your office, I can get it myself. I think I know where my key is," I said.

"Are you going off on your own again?"

"Rose, I know your records are confidential, but I do have a police contract. And if it comes to anything legal, I'll say I broke into your office and stole your Rolodex."

"What are your plans, Gloria?"

It was never easy to derail Rose from her train of thought, I remembered, so I decided to stop trying to distract her and answer her questions as honestly as possible.

"I just need to ask her a few questions about the night of the murder."

"And Matt thinks this is a good idea?"

"Well, he would, but he's too busy to bother with details right now."

"And that's why you're not asking him for the telephone number?"

"Right."

"You're not fooling me, Gloria, but I suppose it's safe for you to talk to an old lady."

"Right," I said again, as if the whole arrangement were Rose's idea.

"If you can't find your key, let me know, and I'll come over."

"No, no, I won't call her till tomorrow anyway."

"I'll call you in the morning when I wake up," Rose said, "and we'll set a time for shopping."

Her voice was trailing off to a whisper as we said good-bye.

As soon as I clicked off my phone, I rummaged around my desk drawer and found the key I had to Rose's office on the second floor. Although I'd let Mrs. Whitestone rest on the evening of her friend's funeral, it wouldn't hurt to have the number handy, I thought.

When I opened the door to my apartment, I saw a long white envelope lying just in front of it. I hadn't heard anyone in the hallway and decided that Galigani's bookkeeper and assistant, Martha, had left it, probably during a loud rendition of "O Come All Ye Faithful." I picked it up and opened it as I headed down the stairs.

I stopped short halfway down to absorb the contents of the note, then turned quickly around, and ran back up the stairs into my apartment. I locked the door behind me and took a deep breath.

Chapter Sixteen

I read the note again. *Dr. Lamerino,* it said, in neat handwriting on ordinary white paper, *you are well-advised to abandon your work on the Hurley investigation.* There was no signature—I'd hoped for "love, Mole"—and no date or other distinguishing mark.

I turned the note over and over as if I could scramble the words and rearrange them into a pleasant greeting, like "Merry Christmas," or "have a nice day." I shivered at the idea that someone had invaded my personal space, which I considered anything above the second floor of the building. Having had my apartment trashed once already, I was doubly sensitive.

I routinely used the Galigani alarm system, but not before I knew I was in for the night. It bothered me to think I'd have to barricade myself in on a routine basis.

After checking my lock two more times, I sat down

and examined the note. The language of the threat, which was how I interpreted the message, intrigued me. The formal grammar and correct spelling were not what I'd expect from Buddy or his friends, if the late Rocky Busso was any example. And not especially Texan, I thought, envisioning the mark of a branding iron and a " 'y'all" if the note had come from William Carey. Patrick Gallagher and Vincent Cavallo, both well educated, were still in the running.

I didn't relish the thought of being a prisoner in my own home, but the idea of venturing out into the mortuary building, dark and empty all around me, was even more unappealing. Tomorrow was soon enough for Frances Whitestone's telephone number, anyway, I reasoned, and I had a freezer full of gourmet ice cream to ease the pain of my captive status.

One more reading of the unsettling note satisfied me that I wasn't in immediate danger, certainly nothing to warrant a call to Matt. I did, however, wish that there could be a cruiser outside my house on a permanent basis.

I took a bowl of Cherry Garcia ice cream and a mug of coffee to my computer. I had some finishing touches to add to my presentation for Peter's class, assuming he was still talking to me. It seemed months since the dramatic flop I'd produced and directed in his faculty lounge, but it was less than twelve hours ago, I realized.

As usual, I found respite from the emotional highs and lows of the week in science. Although it wasn't news to me, I marveled again at the feat of Guglielmo

Marconi, successfully transmitting a signal using radio waves when he was only twenty-one years old.

The outline I'd handed to Peter in draft form still needed attention and I began to fill in a few lines summarizing the contributions of each of the six other scientists on my list. Working alphabetically, a pile of scientific biographies on my lap, I started with a few sentences about the short but brilliant career of Maria Agnesi.

The oldest of twenty-one children, Maria spoke many languages and, at the age of seventeen, wrote a commentary on conic sections. At twenty, she published a volume of one hundred and ninety essays on philosophy, logic, mechanics, and Newton's theory of universal gravitation. Among the essays was a plea for the education of women. I hoped that Peter's students, in the same age range as both Marconi and Agnesi when they did their ground-breaking work, would be inspired.

For the most part, I was comfortable working at my computer, but every now and then I'd hear a noise and feel a twinge of panic. At least three times I tracked down sounds that ended up as refrigerator noise, ice falling from the roof, and steam from the radiator in my bedroom.

I decided to write one more summary, on Avogadro, and then call Elaine in Berkeley, to hear a friendly voice.

Avogadro, unlike the two well-respected child geniuses, received little acceptance as a scientist during his lifetime, but became famous after his death when people realized the importance of his hypotheses. Almost everyone who'd had even an elementary chemistry class knew "Avogadro's number," 602,600,000,000,000,000,000,000, also written, 6.026 $\times$ 10^{23}, the number of particles in a mole of gas.

To give the students an idea of how big Avogadro's number was, I used the standard analogy: if you could count one hundred particles every minute, and counted twelve hours every day and had every person on earth also counting, it would still take more than four million years to count a mole of anything.

A mole of anything. A mole! I came close to shouting "Eureka!" when it hit me. Margaret Hurley had minored in chemistry in college. She would have known Avogadro's number by heart. Even I did, and I'd had only two chemistry classes in my life. I couldn't believe it wasn't the first thing that came to me when I heard "mole." *I've been retired too long,* I thought.

I stood up and paced, back and forth from my computer to my window, recreating the crime scene in my mind. What if Hurley had seen the license plate of the car that was coming toward her, and read 6026 or even 602623, the number including the power of ten? She would have recognized it immediately and made the connection with a mole. One word, mole, was certainly easier to say to the paramedic than the six digits she'd seen.

One problem stood out, however—Massachusetts license plates didn't have four or six digits; they had three digits and three letters. I thought of other possibilities, like an out-of-state car, or a Massachusetts plate with 602, the first part of Avogadro's number, and any three letters. I wondered how to approach Matt on the research that would have to be done to check out my hypothesis. I hoped I wouldn't follow in Avogadro's footsteps and have my theories win acclaim only after my death.

My excitement at determining what I saw as the connection between Margaret Hurley's "mole" and her murderer took over, and my anxiety at the near-ultimatum I'd received on my doorstep all but disappeared. I wanted to share my discovery, but hadn't worked out my strategy for telling Matt. Technically, he'd fired me, I remembered with dismay. Calling Peter was out of the question, and I'd already disturbed Rose sufficiently. It occurred to me that my circle of friends in the Commonwealth of Massachusetts was pitifully small.

I punched in Elaine's number, and got her answering machine. At five o'clock Pacific Standard Time, I pictured her in a traffic jam on Interstate 580—crowded but ice free, I thought.

Finding myself out of ideas for indoor amusement, my only recourse was to leave my apartment. I was sure that whoever left the note in front of my door was long gone, probably thinking I was frightened out of an inclination for further investigation. Nearly correct, I thought, but not quite.

The temperature had risen during the day to the high forties, and it was still above freezing at eight in the evening, so I decided to take a walk. I bundled myself into my new wool jacket, navy blue, hip length, with a serious fleece lining. My winter wardrobe had been enough of a financial commitment to ensure that I'd stay in Revere for at least a few seasons of cold weather. I added boots, scarf, gloves, and a hat, feeling ready to climb an icy peak, and ventured out of the building.

I walked around the bend in Revere Street, past St. Anthony's. I didn't have to enter the church to picture the beautiful Venetian mosaic at the Altar of Our Lady of Perpetual Help, where I'd prayed as a child. I remembered an observation by Niels Bohr, when someone questioned the presence of a horseshoe on a wall in his country cottage. "Can it be that such an eminent physicist believes a horseshoe brings luck?" the guest had asked. "Of course not," Bohr is said to have replied, "but I understand it brings you luck whether you believe or not." *Maybe the same is true of prayer,* I thought.

I headed for the beach, experimenting on the way. Each time a car passed with its headlights facing me, I looked at the license plate to test my hypothesis about Margaret Hurley's mole. I knew that no streetlights were working on Oxford Park on the night of the murder, so I chose the darkest places I could find on Revere Street for test sites. I also took data both with and without the flashlight I'd brought.

I managed to convince myself that I could read a plate, green letters and numbers on a white background, at a distance of between ten and fifteen feet. Of course, I was looking at an angle, and wondered how different it would be if the car were approaching me head-on. Would my brain just click off and not register any information? More important, what did Hurley's brain do?

Distracted by my measurement task, I made it all the way to Revere Beach Boulevard, which runs along the ocean for more than three miles, and is never without traffic. Even in the dead of winter, the ocean's roar competes with the noise from cars and motorcycles, and its salty smell mingles with that of roast beef and fried clams from Kelly's takeout counter.

For a few minutes, I watched a man comb the frosty sand with a metal detector, and a young couple run along the water's edge. I wondered if anyone could stand at that spot and not think about life and death.

I hadn't counted on the return trip when I'd mentally calculated how far I could walk in forty-degree weather. I picked up my pace to keep warm, and had a hard time resisting the more than half a dozen neon invitations from pizza parlors. I was colder than I'd been in many years, and the walk back to my apartment seemed interminable.

When I finally entered my building, my eyes watery and my face and fingers numb, I walked up the main stairs and into my apartment quickly, checking for more unsolicited mail.

I kept on most of my outer clothing while I prepared fresh coffee and toast from a loaf of Italian bread that I had in the freezer. The smells and the steam from the kettle worked their magic and after a few minutes I had the confidence to remove my jacket.

I was also cheered by a blinking red "2" on my answering machine, and pushed PLAY while I made what could be called my dinner if you didn't count the ice cream I'd had earlier.

I heard Elaine's voice first.

"I missed you today," she said. "We went to Bobby's for the department party this afternoon. At least it's December."

Elaine and I joked about how the Christmas parties at our lab started earlier and earlier every year, sometimes barely clearing Thanksgiving.

"I'll be home all evening, so call me."

"I'll be happy to," I told her machine voice, and waited for the second message, which turned out to be not so welcome.

Peter, from my own time zone, had also called while I was out. Since it was nearly ten o'clock it would have made more sense to call him first, but I needed warmth and friendliness more than bickering, so I punched in Elaine's number.

"I think I have a breakthrough," I told her, walking her through my Avogadro's number theory.

"Wow," she said, "you're good, Gloria," and I knew why I'd called Elaine first. I told her my dilemma about the Massachusetts system of three digits, three letters.

"Maybe rental cars have different sets of characters. I know they do in some states. I think it was in Virginia where I was once, and all the rentals started with R."

''Good idea, Elaine, you should come here and be my partner.''

The image of William Carey, the out-of-towner, came to my mind, and I found it easy to picture him behind the wheel of the car that killed Margaret Hurley. I added the rental car idea to my list for Matt. It felt good to think that I might be earning my stipend.

I kept Elaine talking as long as I could, hoping it would be too late to call Peter, and the strategy worked. It was nearly eleven when we wrapped up our stories, and if Peter held to the same schedule he'd had as a young man, he'd be in bed by now.

Before I went to my bedroom, I looked at my unwelcome letter of warning again. It didn't sound like William Carey, nor the somewhat scattered receptionist I'd met at his Chelsea plant. Maybe the Texas drawl was a cover, I thought.

Reviewing my hate mail wasn't conducive to restful sleep, and for a long time I tossed around my bed, trying to insert a picture of Matt Gennaro where now there was only an angry Peter Mastrone, a murderous William Carey, and a dead Rocky Busso.

Chapter Seventeen

After another night of fitful sleep, during which I dreamed I was run over by a mail truck, I rated my week on the Hurley case twice as stressful as the week before my doctoral exams.

I brought a mug of coffee into bed around seven o'clock and started my day by punching in Peter's number. He was always more cheerful in the morning, I remembered, even if I wasn't.

"I'm sorry it was too late to return your call last night," I said.

"Out with the cop?" Peter asked, shooting holes in my theory about his morning mood.

"Peter, I'm sorry about yesterday morning. I know it was very awkward for you."

"It was. But it's not as though Gallagher and I were thick, anyway. Don't worry about it."

"Thanks," I said, almost disappointed at Peter's

civil response. It gave me no excuse to tell him I didn't want to see him for another thirty years.

"I called last night to see if you were free for dinner, but obviously you weren't."

"I walked to the beach, on the spur of the moment," I told him, feeling that, as such a good sport for once, he deserved the truth.

"In this weather? Gloria, you're not in California anymore."

And what a shame, I thought, but not because of the weather. So far, Peter was the only one who could provoke me to regret returning to Revere.

"Peter, I'm sure you have to run. I'll see you Monday. The class is coming along fine."

"Oh, I also wanted to tell you that one of the girls in my class built a radio for a science project, using crystals or something, and she wants to bring it on Monday to show you. I thought you'd be pleased."

"How exciting," I said, noting Peter's emphasis on "girl." "I'll work it into my talk."

"How about a little Christmas lunch on Saturday?"

"I thought we were doing that on Monday."

"Monday's rushed now. I found out I have a faculty meeting in the afternoon."

Before I realized it, I'd agreed to lunch with Peter on Saturday, thus booking myself a two-date day.

Sitting in bed with my phone on my lap, I wished I'd been brave enough to get Frances Whitestone's telephone number the night before. Eventually, I faced reality, with a heavy sigh, and exchanged my nightgown for the jeans and sweatshirt I'd worn to the beach. I hoped to sneak downstairs before any of the staff arrived, and copy the number from Rose's file.

I made it safely to Rose's desk, an antique from her grandparents' home. Although few clients ever saw Rose's office, it was appointed like the elegant person she was, with heirloom furniture and a beautiful Aubusson carpet. I took her Mont Blanc pen from its mahogany cradle, handling it as if it were expensive labware, and copied the Whitestone number.

I turned to leave and ran head-on into Martha. I was more frightened than I should have been, and poor Martha was full of apologies. She was also wearing jeans and a sweatshirt, and was just as surprised as I was to meet someone on the second floor of the mortuary at seven-thirty in the morning.

"Oh, am I glad it's you," Martha said, echoing my sentiments. "We're all technically off today. I'm on my way to drop the kids off at school, and thought I'd come in and pick up some work to take home. It was such a hectic week."

"It certainly was," I said. "Martha, what time did you leave yesterday?"

"Thursday," she said, frowning and clutching her chin. "I picked up the kids at four-thirty, so I left around four-fifteen. I was supposed to stay till five, but I was exhausted. That's why I came back this morning."

I didn't want Martha to think I was the funeral worker police, so I told her my reason for asking, almost.

"I received a note yesterday from a friend, and I wonder if you saw him deliver it."

"Yes, I did, just before I left. The place was still open and I saw him go upstairs. Very handsome."

Martha's eyebrows went up at "handsome," and I felt obliged to clarify.

"Not that kind of friend, Martha. Did he say anything to you?"

"No, just nodded, polite, seemed in a hurry. I'm glad the sergeant doesn't have any competition. I like him."

"I do, too. Thanks, Martha. I hope you have an easy day today."

Back in my apartment, I made a list of all the men in the Hurley case who I thought Martha would think were handsome, and came up with one: Vincent Cavallo. *Now, if Vincent Cavallo drives a rental car,* I thought, *the case is solved.* It seemed clear to me that Cavallo delivered the letter from his "silent partner." It was time to call Matt.

Fortified by more coffee and scrambled eggs, I called Matt's office, where I pictured him with his customary breakfast bagel.

I gave him the details of my Avogadro breakthrough and he seemed to take it seriously, which pleased me.

"I'll put some people on it," he said. "It beats anything else we've got."

I almost told him about my threatening letter, sitting on my dresser next to the red velvet box Rocky had brought, but in the clear morning light, it didn't seem as threatening, and I didn't want to worry him. Or lose my job.

"No more on Rocky?" I asked.

"We do know he was expecting a large infusion of money. That's about all."

"So, will you let me know how it goes with the license plate?"

"You can read about it in the *Journal.*"

"Matt," I said, with a mock-whiny voice.

"You know I appreciate your insights, Gloria. As long as you keep your body out of the way. Well, you know what I mean."

We both laughed, and I felt another milestone had been reached. First, a playful shoulder gesture, then a body joke. *What progress,* I thought, *and we're only fifty-five years old*. It's a good thing the propagation of the human race didn't depend on us.

I decided that Frances Whitestone didn't count as a danger to my body, and placed my next call to her. I figured I would get her secretary, and had rehearsed my opening lines.

"This is Dr. Gloria Lamerino," I said. "I'm working with the police and I wonder if I might have a few minutes of Mrs. Whitestone's time, at her convenience."

"I'm afraid Mrs. Whitestone is preparing to leave this afternoon for an indefinite period of time. This is her assistant, Mrs. Crawford. Is there something I can do for you?"

"I need only ten or fifteen minutes of her time. Is there any possibility that I can see her this morning?"

"One moment, please."

Mrs. Crawford sounded strangely like someone in an old movie I'd seen, about a deadly housekeeper in an old mansion on a hill. Or maybe it was her name that called up the image.

"Mrs. Whitestone can spare twenty minutes, beginning at nine-thirty."

"Thank you so much. I'll see you then."

I raced around to get ready, checking my closet for an elegant morning look. I put on a dark green paisley skirt, green knit top, and black wool blazer. I chose a long string of onyx beads and opted for once to forego a lapel pin. Mrs. Whitestone hadn't seemed the type to appreciate my collection. I added the several pounds of wool—coat, gloves, scarf, hat—that it would take to keep me comfortable on the walk to Oxford Park, three blocks away.

The inside of the Whitestone house was even more imposing than the outside, with a beautiful carved wood banister on the stairs from the foyer, not unlike the one in the funeral parlor. I guessed they were built around the same time, in the early 1940s.

The artwork in the study, where I waited for Frances Whitestone, was a tribute to Ireland, reminding me of the recent *Globe* piece that profiled her own family— she'd been born Frances Mulrooney. An Irish blessing was embroidered on a banner that hung on one wall, a framed poster of Irish family shields on another. Maps of old and new Ireland lined the walls above built-in bookcases. It was the kind of decor that wouldn't have been out of place in a pub, except that it looked tasteful and expensive, in rich fabrics and inlaid wood.

As Mrs. Whitestone entered the study, her tall, imposing frame seemed to fill the doorway. She wore matching knits, shoes, and scarf in a rich taupe with dull gold accents, and when she greeted me I found myself standing straighter and adjusting the shoulders of my jacket. I wished I'd consulted Rose before coming.

"Thank you for seeing me on such short notice," I said, almost adding "Your Holiness."

Mrs. Whitestone motioned for me to sit on a museumlike chair with a straight back and a stiff satiny cushion on its seat. *No wonder she has such good posture,* I thought. *There's no sinking into this furniture.*

"I saw you at the mortuary, didn't I?" she said to me, giving me the same once-over I'd gotten from her when she'd fretted over the dearth of candles. She seemed very tired, but not about to relinquish the tremendous control she had of her emotions.

"Yes, I'm associated with the Galiganis," I said, becoming quite glib about the many hats I wore lately.

"And with the police? You are versatile for a scientist."

I looked up sharply, catching Mrs. Whitestone's cold green eyes. She gave me a thin smile, and I felt a slight wave of fear. Did all the principals in the Hurley case know more about me than I knew about them, I wondered, and how did Mrs. Whitestone come to be in charge of this interview? I'd almost forgotten the line of questioning I'd prepared for.

For support, I took out my notebook.

"I'd like to ask you about Margaret's brother, Brendan, Mrs. Whitestone," I said. "I didn't have a chance to talk with him during the wake."

I waited, but Mrs. Whitestone remained virtually motionless, her hands on her lap, except that I could almost see the workings of her busy head. I hadn't actually asked a question, I realized, and she had no comment. I couldn't bring myself to ask her directly what she thought of Buddy's chances of inheriting his father's money now that Margaret was dead. Facing her, I lost all courage to ask any bold question, and I heard myself imitate television detectives.

"Did you see anything unusual on your street last Sunday?"

"No."

"How many people knew Margaret's schedule and when she might be arriving on Oxford Park?"

"I knew it, and probably some of my acquaintances, and anyone whom Margaret herself told."

"I'm trying to track down a license plate," I said, aware that my so-called interview had no focus. I gave her the number I was interested in, eliminating mention of how I arrived at it.

This time she chose to answer a question with a question.

"Aren't the police handling all this?"

"I'd hoped to be of some help, Mrs. Whitestone.

We're all as anxious as you are to find Margaret's murderer.''

''I have put my confidence in the police department, Dr. Lamerino, and I suggest you do the same.''

''I understand you're not happy with how they're handling Margaret's personal effects.''

''That's true. I can't understand what the police can possibly get from a garment bag and a few Christmas presents.''

At that, Mrs. Whitestone stood up, and at the same time, Mrs. Crawford entered the study with my coat. I checked my watch—nine-fifty. My audience was over.

On the walk home I reviewed my progress, which I graded harshly. I'd flunked interview techniques with Patrick Gallagher and Frances Whitestone, got nothing significant from William Carey, feared Rocky Busso unnecessarily, and been frightened into captivity by Vincent Cavallo.

It seemed that there was nothing for me to do but wait for the results of the license-plate trace. Having failed at police work, I was ready to take on shopping again, so as soon as I'd shed my outer clothes, I called Rose.

''Are you awake?'' I asked her.

''I was just going to call you. I'm ready to stop being lazy. What have you been doing?''

''I just dropped in on Frances Whitestone,'' I said.

''Already?''

"She's going out of town today, so I got in just in time."

"Actually, I'm surprised she's still around, with bad memories right at her doorstep," Rose said. "Margaret was the closest thing Frances had to a granddaughter. If something like that happened to me, I'd split for another state immediately. And she's the one who can do it—the Whitestones have houses all over New England. For that matter, so do the Hurleys—what's left of them."

"Hmm," I said. "Do you think they have cars all over New England, too?"

Chapter Eighteen

It was too awful a thought to entertain for very long—Buddy murdering his own sister. I still had no firsthand knowledge of him and it was hard not to be swayed by his media image, a gambler from a rich and powerful family, with gangster buddies. I resolved to try to sweet-talk Matt into telling me at least the status of the Hurley estate with Margaret out of the picture.

But, for the moment, I had serious shopping to do, and Rose cooperated by picking me up and driving us into Boston. Her reasoning was that we'd be carrying home too many packages to make a subway trip feasible.

With only about two weeks until Christmas, I had to make a big dent in my shopping list, at least for the people in California. I'd already called for rates for overnight delivery, and hoped I didn't have to use the service. Rose helped me choose a silk scarf with a beige print, and a gold circle pin from the Museum of Fine Arts Design School, both for Elaine. I picked up sweatshirts with ''Boston'' and ''Quincy Market'' logos for several other Berkeley friends, and bought odds and ends of decorations for my apartment.

''Now for the hard part,'' I said, looking at the window display in a men's store on Tremont Street.

''Matt?''

''Matt and Peter.''

To my surprise, I found it as difficult to choose a present for someone I didn't care about as for one I liked a lot. I didn't want to give either man the wrong impression, and in Matt's case, I wasn't even sure what the right impression was.

Rose cleared her throat in a way that I recognized as the signal for a revelation or confession of some sort.

''Peter called me,'' she said.

''And?''

''He wanted my advice on a present for you.''

''Should I be worried?''

''Not anymore. I talked him out of a heart-shaped locket. I told him I didn't think it was you, and that he should consider a gift certificate to Borders Books and Music.''

I breathed a sigh of relief into the cold air and watched it fill the space between us.

''Thank you, thank you,'' I said, hugging my friend as we walked along the edge of Boston Common.

The temperature had been rising one or two degrees

every day throughout the week, and the warmer weather had created a patchwork design on the Common. Rose and I left our footprints in the interlocking squares of dirty snow and brown grass in front of the State House.

We stopped for coffee and talked about what we'd wear on our double date the next night, and for a while we were young girlfriends at Revere High School again, the reality of an unsolved murder drifting very far way.

"We need to find you something in red or green," Rose said. "You can't wear black all the time."

"I have some clothes that aren't black."

"Even the ones that aren't black might as well be."

"What does that mean?"

"Let's go to Copley Place and I'll show you what I mean."

We laughed and put on our coats, ready for the next round.

By the time we were finished for the day, I'd bought myself a *Messiah* outfit—a calf-length green velvet dress with three-quarter sleeves, and black patent flats with a sling back. I'd rejected the same style in three-inch heels. As we piled ourselves and our bundles into Rose's station wagon, I tried to ignore the neatly folded white curtains she kept in the trunk in case the car was pressed into service to pick up a client.

I'd bought a coffee-table book on the wonders of Italy for Peter, an electronic address book that dialed a telephone, for Frank, and all my California gifts. Rose had bags of stocking stuffers for her children and grandson, since, as usual, she had bought and wrapped most of her major gifts before Thanksgiving. I still had nothing for Matt.

We drove home to Frank, who'd used his rare day off to prepare a meal for the three of us—a dish he called eggplant Galigani, with polenta and eggplant and roasted peppers. He seemed pleased with his efforts, and we gave him enough praise to ensure a repeat performance. Until I met Matt, I'd never cared about being "the odd person," even when visiting couples in California, but lately I'd found myself wanting to share moments like eggplant Galigani with him.

I left the Galigani home early, hoping to get my first reasonable night's sleep in almost a week. I wasn't sure whether it was Frank's culinary talent or the shopping bags piled around my bedroom that gave me comfort, but I managed to fall asleep quickly, with no nightmares that I could remember the next morning.

My Saturday seemed out of my hands—I'd have to wrap presents before and after lunch with Peter, and get ready for dinner and the *Messiah* concert. With no decisions to make, and the mindless task of stretching jolly paper and ribbon around boxes, my brain was free to draw up lists and make connections among all the fuzzy bits of data on the Hurley case.

I still considered the most promising line the one from Vincent Cavallo to his "partner" and the partner's out-of-state car. My best guess was that Buddy

Hurley was the partner—he could have hired Busso to kill Margaret, then killed Busso to cover himself—but I had nothing concrete to back it up.

I tried to push the whole case out of my head as I sang along with Barbra Streisand, wondering who had talked a Jewish woman into making a Christmas album.

I dressed casually for lunch with Peter, partly because it was Saturday and partly to diminish the importance of the event. As I pulled on my black wool pants, I admitted to myself another reason—I knew Peter still preferred dresses and skirts on women.

Once again fully wrapped in my new winter clothes, I went to the garage, coming upon Guido, the sweet young student from Italy who cleaned the building on Saturday mornings. Whenever we met, Guido and I had a routine exchange of Italian, during which I practiced the language I was once fluent in.

"Buon giorno," I said.

"Che porta?" Guido asked, pointing to the large, gaily wrapped book I had for Peter.

"Una cosa per natale," I said, using the ridiculous phrase, "a thing for Christmas," since I didn't know the word for "present."

Guido always gave me a thumbs-up anyway, no matter how poorly I responded.

Peter had chosen Russo's café, near the center of town, where the police station, Revere City Hall, the main post office, and the *Journal* office all sat within not more than a hundred yards of each other.

The first thing that worried me when I saw Peter, already sipping a mocha, was the tiny box near his napkin. It looked more the right size for a locket than for a gift certificate. *Not off to a great start,* I thought, *and so much for Rose's powers of persuasion.*

"I've ordered an antipasto, and the pasta primavera for both of us," Peter said, and even that annoyed me, as just another sign of his male chauvinist attitudes. And I was going to have to choose between Russo's delicious, delicately fried zucchini and making a feminist statement by fasting.

I barely focused on our conversation during the meal, distilling phrases like "more of each other in the new year" and "so much to catch up on." I concentrated on my pasta, glancing now and then at the tiramisu in the pastry case.

"Present time!" Peter announced, with a big smile.

I took a deep breath and handed Peter's package across the table.

He put the short edge on his lap, leaned on it, and handed me the small box.

"You first," I said, hoping Peter would see the trend, take back the box, and pull a gift certificate out of his pocket.

Peter opened his package carefully, as if he intended to use the paper and the cellophane tape again.

"You can exchange it for something else if you already have it," I said as he was lifting the book from its wrapper. What I meant was, "this gift has no personal significance, and is interchangeable with all the other gifts in the world."

He seemed pleased with the wonders of Italy and assured me that he didn't already have a copy and that he'd been wanting one.

There was no more stalling; it was my turn. I tore the paper off the small box. I had a strange recollection of opening the box Rocky Busso had handed me not so long ago.

On a bed of white silk I saw a gold heart-shaped pendant, about two centimeters down the middle. At least it wasn't a locket with his photo in it, I thought, trying to smile at the same time.

"This is beautiful, Peter. Thank you."

"I wanted to get you something special."

"Peter . . ."

"Don't say anything, Gloria. I know you've been busy and haven't had time for socializing, but as I said a few minutes ago, I hope that'll change in the new year."

"I don't—"

"Why don't we wait till all this holiday rush is over and spend some time together. I'll be gone for two weeks, and when I come back—"

It was my turn to interrupt, and it took a giant effort for me not to scream.

"Peter, I can't see us ever spending a lot of time together," I said. "I hope we can be friends without complicating things."

Peter's jaw stiffened as he pinched his eyes closed and breathed in deeply.

"I don't want to hear this now," he said. "I have

a meeting this afternoon, and there's no time to really talk.''

He looked at his watch and signaled for the check. I thought about making a move to pay my share, but felt I'd done enough damage to Peter for one holiday season. He left bills on the table and stood up. Without my noticing, he'd managed to rewrap his book with no detectable wrinkles. He tucked it under his arm and leaned over to kiss me on the forehead.

"Sorry I have to run," he said. "I'll see you on Monday."

I ordered another coffee and sat at the table for a while, wondering what made people like Peter tick. We certainly had different responses to rejection. Whenever anyone expressed the slightest displeasure with me, I backed away immediately, apologizing for being in the way. Josephine's training, I realized, and couldn't fault it.

I got home about two o'clock and did something rare for me—I started to lay out my clothes for the evening. *Rose would be proud of me,* I thought; *I'm practicing dating behavior.* I was smoothing out the folds of my new dress when I stopped to answer my telephone, hoping it wasn't Peter.

I heard a muffled voice against a background of traffic.

"This is Vincent Cavallo," he said. "I have some information you might want on the Hurley murder investigation."

"What is it?" I asked, clutching the phone, as if that would keep my informant on the line.

"Not now. I'm calling from a pay phone near City Hall. Can you meet me somewhere?"

I didn't relish the thought of going all the way back down Broadway again, but I couldn't pass up a chance for information. And I certainly would be safe out in public, even if Cavallo were setting me up. I looked at the clock. Matt was to pick me up at six. As long as I was back by five-fifteen, I'd have plenty of time to get into my new dress and shoes.

"I'll meet you at Luberto's in twenty minutes," I said, seeing nothing wrong with combining a Deep Throat meeting with a pastry run. I'd wanted to have something to go with coffee after the concert anyway.

I drove to Luberto's, arriving about three o'clock, and took a seat at a small table near the back of the shop. I ordered a cappuccino and gave the clerk a list of sweets to package for me.

More than an hour later, I was still waiting for Cavallo. It had already turned dark, and I'd finished my *Scientific American*. I couldn't imagine what had gone wrong. The worst thing I could think of was that he was the third victim in the Hurley case.

I picked up my box of pastry and left the shop. As I unlocked my car, something in the window of a store near where I was parked caught my eye. *Luggage sale,* the sign said, and under it was a garment bag.

How could I have been so dumb? I asked myself. As I drove home, I saw how the clues added up. Number one, Mrs. Whitestone had complained to me that the police still had Margaret's garment bag, but the police had told no one about the luggage. She couldn't have known about the bag unless she drove the car herself, or learned about it later from Rocky, probably while she was forcing him to write his confession to the murder.

Number two, I finally realized, was that Margaret had not been calling for Mrs. Whitestone, as the paramedic thought. She had been naming her killer, since she recognized the license plate. No wonder Mrs. Whitestone insisted on talking to everyone who had access to Margaret before she died.

Number three, Mrs. Whitestone had the money to be Cavallo's "partner," and therefore also the motive to kill to protect her interests.

I planned to report to Matt as soon as I got to my apartment, skipping the part where I went on a wild goose chase to meet Cavallo.

My only question was whether Mrs. Whitestone was so ruthless that she would have her friend and protégé murdered for the sake of her investments.

I pulled into the mortuary garage, entered the foyer, and came face-to-face with Frances Whitestone. One look at her, gun in hand, and I had my answer.

Chapter Nineteen

I stood in my foyer, holding my box of Italian desserts. Mrs. Whitestone seemed to tower over me more than ever.

"How did you get in?" I asked, as if logistics were all that mattered. She was wearing a long, dark brown coat with a high fur collar, and for a moment I convinced myself that the gun in her hand was merely an extension of her tasteful brown leather gloves.

"It's astounding what people will do for a helpless old lady," she said, standing straight as ever, not a hair out of place. "A man in overalls let me in earlier so I could pick up more of my dear departed friend's holy cards. For all he knows, I left the building before he did."

Guido, I said to myself. *E dove sta? Where are you now?*

"Cavallo set me up," I said, to myself and my intruder, unable to turn off my brain and face the danger my body was in.

"You went out to do an errand and were unfortunate enough to meet a prowler in the foyer."

"You can't do this," I heard myself say, as if I were talking to the schoolyard bully. "I have a date with a homicide detective. He'll be here any minute."

"Your detective has been called out unexpectedly, to trace a lead he can't refuse. On the Hurley case," she said, with a thin smile.

"The police know about your out-of-state license plate." *True to form,* I told myself, *you think you can argue your way through life.*

"Poor Margaret loved that license plate. She noticed the significance right away and was so proud of herself. Anyway, that's already been taken care of. How difficult do you think it was to wipe out one little record—especially since I own that little New Hampshire town?"

I searched around my brain for more reasons why she shouldn't add me to her list of victims. I was ridiculously embarrassed to be intimidated by a woman old enough to be my mother, but she was taller and she had a gun. My only advantage was that she seemed to want to chat before she shot me, and I had the feeling that she wanted to tell me something I didn't know yet.

"Guido will remember you," I said, "and the police will figure it out."

"The police give up easily, unlike you. I told Al years ago that you would be trouble."

My eyes must have widened considerably, and I finally dropped the box of pastries I'd been holding. Mrs. Whitestone smiled, and I knew she was pleased at the effect her words had on me.

"Al? You knew Al Gravese?"

"Al and Margaret were a lot alike. First, they were too idealistic for the real world, then they took what they could get. But they were weak. They had qualms of conscience. They didn't understand you can't go back."

"You had Al killed, too," I said, my voice weak and hoarse at the stunning revelation of how far back into my youth this woman's power reached.

"You're a lot like me," Mrs. Whitestone said. "An intelligent woman. Strong-minded. Not easily intimidated. Under different circumstances, we could have been great friends."

Mrs. Whitestone must have been insulted by my wide-eyed, skeptical response to her compliment, because her eyes narrowed and she tightened her grip on the gun. I knew if I were going to act at all, this was the time.

I made a quick calculation of the length of the strap on my purse, hanging from my right shoulder, and flung the purse at Mrs. Whitestone with all my strength. She reeled backward, banging into the stairway banister, the gun falling from her hand, but it was still too far away for me to reach.

For once, carrying the huge leather sack around had given me an advantage, I thought. Even in the midst of panic, I wished I could call Elaine, whose purse was a small, classy fashion statement, and tell her she was right—my purse was a weapon, heavy enough to ward off an attacker.

I doubted that I could get past Mrs. Whitestone to the outside door. She was closer to the gun than I was, even if she was a little off-balance. I ran to the nearest inside door, which lead to the stairs to the basement.

My worst moments at Galigani's seemed to be at the extremes of the building—first in the attic, where I was shot at, and now in the basement. I wished I'd spent more time here so I'd know my options better.

The laundry room had a window to the outside, but it was so small only a child could fit through it. The prep room, a "dead end" one might say, had no windows. I thought of the tour Frank had given me when I first moved into the mortuary, and remembered a host of potential weapons in the form of embalming tools. I shuddered as I pictured the trocar, three feet long, with a razor-sharp point, used to remove excess fluid from his deceased clients. I wondered if I had the courage to use it on a live person, even if my own life depended on it.

I went into the prep room and locked the door behind me, grateful that there were no clients on this Saturday afternoon. I thought about hiding—climbing onto a table and covering myself with a cloth, crawling into a cabinet under the sink. None of the options seemed feasible.

I was even more disheartened when I noticed the elevator, which I'd forgotten about. Galigani's rickety old elevator ran through the middle of the building, from the second floor to the basement, opening onto the landing at the top end, and directly into the prep room at the bottom end.

I had no idea what Mrs. Whitestone's condition was upstairs, or whether she'd noticed the elevator doors. If I could be sure she wasn't on it, I could call the elevator down, and hold it open in the basement. Then I'd just have to spend the rest of the weekend in the prep room until someone came in on Monday. Unless, of course, someone died in the meantime.

I looked above the elevator door at the old-fashioned semicircular brass plate, and saw its arrow pointing to 2. If I called the car down, Mrs. Whitestone would hear it, and I couldn't be sure the car wouldn't stop for her if she pushed the button. So far, I'd heard no noise in the elevator shaft.

A moment later, I did hear a noise, but it was the doorknob rattling and I felt a shiver of panic, even though I knew the door to the stairway was locked. There was no window on the door, so I could only imagine an angry Mrs. Whitestone standing there, having recovered her balance and her gun.

This would make a good problem in a physics book, I thought, as if I knew no fear. Will the elevator car, now on the second floor, pass the first floor before Mrs. Whitestone, now in the basement, can get back to the first floor and push the button? Impossible to figure without knowing the speed of the elevator car, I concluded. I'd only been on it once before, without a stopwatch. And who could estimate the speed of a woman who was already responsible for three deaths that I knew of?

I pulled myself together. Redundancy, that was it. Years of lab work taught me the importance of backup systems and plan B arrangements: *Call the elevator,* I decided, pushing the button at that very moment, *and also be prepared for attack if Mrs. Whitestone arrives in the basement.*

Keeping my eye on the arrow, making its way slowly to the first floor, I looked around the prep room, more impressed than ever at its cleanliness and neatness. I wished I'd paid more attention to Frank when he showed me around. Where were the knives, scissors, and saws when I needed them?

I opened the drawers under the counters, two at a time. Nothing sharp, nothing heavy, certainly no gun. Was everything in the shop for repairs? I wondered. I looked up at the wall above the elevator; the arrow had stopped at 1.

Moving as quickly as I could, feeling my rapid heart beat in the vicinity of my throat, I pulled open the cabinets and found one filled with clear bottles of liquid. I invoked the memory of my high-school chemistry teacher and chose one labeled DRYENE. It had the biggest skull-and-crossbones symbol of them all, and a special orange wrapper that read *For Cauterizing Wounds.*

I carried the bottle back to the elevator, unscrewing the black plastic top. The arrow was rotating slowly clockwise, coming close to its rest position, B. I pressed myself against the wall, flush with the elevator doors, so that I'd be on Mrs. Whitestone's right when she exited the car. I'd figured that would give her the least effective angle for shooting with her right hand.

I heard the car hit bottom. An old lady or an empty car? I wondered, as I practiced flicking my wrist, hoping I could manage exactly the angle for Mrs. Whitestone's face. Except that I couldn't think of it as Mrs. Whitestone's face. I couldn't think at all; I just had to do it.

The elevator doors opened and I smelled Mrs. Whitestone's expensive perfume. *If you're on a mission to kill someone,* I thought, *shouldn't you be fragrance-free?* Either because I was lucky, or because I wasn't wearing any telltale scent, Mrs. Whitestone turned first to her left as she entered the prep room.

I had my arm in position for a wide swing. I gave the bottle of acid a large rotational momentum upward, allowing for Mrs. Whitestone's height, then tipped it so that a stream of clear, caustic liquid hit her forehead and streamed down her face. I was nearly sick at the sight of it, and at the idea of it.

She screamed, dropping the gun and pressing the palms of her hands to her face. I kicked the gun as far across the room as I could, then ran out the door to the stairs and outside.

I ran along Tuttle Street, not looking back. There were no phone booths in my immediate neighborhood and I didn't think of stopping at any of the homes on the street. I didn't think of stopping at all, not knowing where Mrs. Whitestone was, and not wanting to find out. I ran for several blocks, a personal best.

In one of the universe's marvelous displays of symmetry, a cruiser was parked at the edge of Oxford Park. I ran to it, cheered by the red, white, and blue of Revere's Pride.

"I just attacked someone," I said, falling onto the hood of the police car as if I'd been busted and told to spread my legs.

Later I remembered seeing Matt, not knowing how either of us got there, to the corner of Revere Street and Oxford Park, not understanding why he was so dressed up. I didn't recognize the suit he was wearing, a striking navy blue, nor the scarf, which was a dazzling blue-and-beige paisley.

When it came to me that this was my date for the evening, who'd come to pick me up, I sobbed.

"I'm so sorry," I said. "Are we missing the concert?"

"We'll catch it next year," Matt said, cradling my head as we sat in the back of the cruiser, "and the next, and the next after that."

Chapter Twenty

We were at the end of the first and very successful party in my apartment—Christmas brunch for the extended Galigani family, Matt, and me. I'd accepted help all around, remaining responsible only for decorations and one main dish—a frittata—in spite of Josephine's reproachful voice. I couldn't remember any guests ever bringing food or drink into Josephine's house.

The present exchange between Matt and me went much better than I'd hoped for. We were on the same wavelength, each giving the other a gift of time. I'd found a roundabout way, through a California friend, to get coveted tickets for a January concert in Harvard Square by one of Matt's favorite jazz artists. He presented me with tickets for a series of four all-Beethoven concerts at Symphony Hall. I'd folded his tickets inside a new blue scarf, to replace the one I'd been slightly sick on two weeks before. He'd tucked mine into a small black satin evening purse with a note that said *Not for use as a weapon.*

The Galigani children, spouses, and grandson had gone on to other celebrations, and the four of us who were left sat listening to soft Christmas piano music, suitable for full stomachs. Parts of the newspaper were handed around and we chatted and read together.

"I still can't believe Frances Whitestone," Rose said, finishing an article in the newspaper. "How can anyone have a close friend murdered?"

"I guess 'close' means something different to the rich and powerful," Frank said.

"She had a lot of money and power tied up in helium," I said, "going all the way back to the Sixties." I pushed back images of Frances Whitestone, ambushing me in my foyer, aiming a gun at me, and screaming in the prep room.

"I hear she's regained the sight in one eye," Matt said, with a glance at me that said, "so don't feel guilty."

"Plus, she has a few scars and some bad press that she deserves," Frank said.

Although I hadn't yet expressed it, I was distressed that a physicist had also been involved in illegal dealings—Vincent Cavallo was to be indicted for fraud. In my mind scientists ranked next to little old ladies for purity of heart.

Rose walked over to me and put her arms around me. "I can't stand these close calls, Gloria. I can't imagine what I'd do without you."

"I don't have a scratch this time," I said, holding out my arms for inspection, as if she could see through my new green velvet dress.

"And we're going to keep it that way," Matt said.

"I hope that doesn't mean I'm fired."

"It means we're going to meet less often at my office and more often at parties."

We raised our various glasses and mugs to cheer Matt's pronouncement. Moments later Rose had retrieved two coats from the closet and tugged at Frank's arm. She made "let's leave them alone" gestures which Frank seemed to understand immediately.

Matt and I were due on the Cape around four o'clock for dinner with his sister's family. I'd never met them, and I was a bit anxious as I packed up the presents and food we were taking with us.

At the last minute, I dug my camera out of my dresser drawer.

"Do you think they'd mind if I take photos?" I asked.

"Not at all. The kids love to show off."

I opened the back of the camera to insert new film.

"This camera is so old," I said. "I'm dying to get a new one, with lithium batteries."

"Oh, no," Matt said, giving me a menacing grin as he moved closer.

It's a good thing I hadn't misinterpreted his move to kiss me, because I met him more than halfway.